I0580899

Murder Sometimes Cold

Also By Murray Moffatt

A Different Kind of Life (Autobiography)

Play

**Murder Best Unsolved*

**Murder Maybe Relative*

**Murder Maybe By Evil*

Murder And No Play

**Murder Sometimes Cold*

**A Shane Daniels Murder Mystery*

Murder Sometimes Cold

A Shane Daniels Murder Mystery

A Novel by

Murray Moffatt

ISBN: 978-1-7782065-4-2

Author's Note:

When I completed my second novel, "Murder Best Unsolved", I thought that would be the end of my relationship with Shane Daniels.

However, when I came up with an idea for another murder mystery and I needed someone to solve it, I realized that Shane and his partner Emma would be a perfect fit with their combination of smarts and desire to always do the right thing.

And there's more to it than just that. Shane had some unresolved personal issues that I wanted to explore even further, including his complicated relationship with his father who was serving a life sentence for murder.

Plus, it's fun writing about a character who is tall, dark and handsome, my complete opposite. So, Shane has become my go to guy and is back in our fourth novel together.

I hope you enjoy following Shane as he tries to solve two murders.

Once again, I want to extend a sincere thank you to everyone who has taken the time to read my novels and for the support and encouragement of my retirement hobby.

A special thank you to my wonderful wife Jill who does the thankless job of proofreading my work and to my daughters, Sarah and Laura, for their love and support.

This is a work of fiction. Names, characters, places and incidents are all products of my imagination. Any resemblance to actual events, locations, organizations or persons, living or dead, is entirely coincidental. Any mistakes are mine alone.

For my father Dalton Moffatt

My Dad was the complete opposite of the fathers in this story. He was a principled man dedicated to his family.

I wish he was still here.

"People don't remember. Revenge is sweet"
Tracey Emin (British artist)

"The point is you can't be too greedy"
Donald Trump

"Greed is so destructive. It destroys everything"
Eartha Kitt

Prologue

When I look back over the events of my latest case, which nearly cost the life of an important person in my life, I keep thinking about the saying, "Revenge is a dish best served cold".

For some reason, I always thought the phrase was from one of Shakespeare's plays, but the nerd in me had to know for sure so I put it in Google and I found out I was wrong.

It's believed the phrase was first used by French author Eugene Sue in his book, "Memories of Matilda" published in 1844, but an English translation that was done two years later has the actual quote as "And then revenge is very good eaten cold as the vulgar say".

The first time I heard a variation of the saying was in 'The Godfather', the 1972 movie that I consider the best American film ever made, and one I've watched so many times I have most of the dialogue memorized.

In the film, mafia boss Don Corleone says, "Revenge is a dish that tastes best when it is cold". The phrase was even used by the evil superhuman Khan in 1982's Star Trek II, 'The Wrath of Khan'.

The events of the past several weeks also have me thinking about the difference between avenge and revenge, and again the nerd in me had to do some research. My partner, Emma, told me I was probably obsessing over this stuff as a way of dealing with what happened.

The consensus I found on Google was that to avenge is to punish a wrong, while revenge is harsher and less concerned with justice than with retaliating by inflicting harm. So, revenge generally means the act of taking vengeance for injuries or wrongs. Avenge, on the other hand, has more to do with seeking justice or retribution for someone other than ourselves.

Anyone who knows me knows that I'm a fan of Westerns and my father, also a huge fan of the genre, named me after the main character in the classic 1953 film, 'Shane', starring Alan Ladd. I don't know how many times my father told me he actually wanted to name me 'Duke' in honour of John Wayne, but my mother wouldn't allow it.

If you watch enough Westerns, you realize that many of their plots are built around revenge or avenge; the cowboy hero sets out on his horse to track down the bad guys responsible for killing his wife or maybe his best friend. The older the film, the greater the chance the climax involves a showdown between the good guy and the bad guy. The hero gets his revenge.

In Clint Eastwood's 1992 academy award-winning film, 'Unforgiven', he portrays a retired gunslinger who agrees to go after the bounty offered by a group of prostitutes who want revenge on the man who mutilated one of their group.

Even in one of my favourite Westerns, 1993's 'Tombstone' starring Kurt Russell, it's all about revenge. In this case, famous lawman Wyatt Earp, played by Russell, seeks out and kills members of the red sash-wearing cowboy gang responsible for killing his brother Morgan and maiming his other brother, Virgil.

I know about vengeance from my own life and I'm not particularly proud of it. I almost killed my father to avenge his part in the death of my mother and for murdering a woman I had become romantically involved with.

I was eighteen years old when I started having sex with Alina Ivanov, a young, beautiful Russian immigrant who lived in my hometown of Paisley, a village in southwestern Ontario. She was married to another Russian, Max Ivanov, and shortly after we began our affair, she disappeared. I eventually proved she had been murdered after finding her body in a shallow grave in a wooded area outside of Paisley. Max was sentenced to life for the murder, but that was only the beginning of the story.

It turned out that Max was my uncle, he and my father were adopted separately from a Moscow orphanage, and more than a decade after he was sent to prison, he confessed to me that he didn't kill Alina, my father did. Max claimed he actually killed my mother as part of an agreement he made with my father after they discovered they were brothers.

I didn't believe Max, who told me this because he was dying and wanted to clear his conscious, because I loved my father and had never questioned his explanation that my mother had abandoned us when I was very young and he didn't know where she had gone. I had wonderful memories of my mother, but couldn't understand why she left me, and over the years my father deflected my attempts to get him to explain what happened.

Although I chose not to believe what Max told me, I couldn't let it go, and with the help of my childhood friend, Ben Chen, went back to the woods where I dug up Alina's body and found where Max had buried my mother's remains.

I confronted my father at the home where I grew up in Paisley and he admitted that what Max claimed was true. Max had killed my mother because my father was angry about her many affairs with men around Paisley and he didn't want to lose half his business if he divorced her.

Years later, my father agreed to kill Alina because Max was angry about her infidelity. My father was aware Alina and I were friends and that I had feelings for her, but he didn't care, went to her house, strangled her, and buried her in the woods, not far from where Max put my mother.

When my father confessed, I was beside myself with anger and immediately wanted vengeance for what he had done. I started strangling him with every intention of ending his life and the only reason I stopped was because I heard Emma in my mind saying, "Shane, come back!", quoting the famous line from the movie, just as she did when I had left our Brantford home for Paisley to see my father. I would likely be in prison today, just like my father, if not for hearing Emma's words.

I also know what it feels like to want revenge.

I had always dreamed about being a cop, with the goal of eventually a Detective, and that came true when I was hired by the Brantford Police Service. But that career came to an early and sudden end when my Training Officer and I attended a domestic dispute involving a couple who had been drinking heavily. The husband tried to shoot his wife with a shotgun, but I pushed her out of the way and was hit in the left knee, destroying it. My dream career was over before it had hardly started, I was permanently disabled and now walk with the aid of a cane.

The night of the incident, the man with the shotgun fired at my Training Officer hitting him in the chest, but he was luckily saved by his bulletproof vest. I then shot the drunken man, killing him instantly.

I honestly never felt remorse for killing that man, but the loss of my career and the constant pain in my ravaged knee put me in a downward spiral of booze and pills. I admit that during that time period, I thought a lot about getting revenge on the wife of the man I shot. As far as I was concerned, she was just as much to blame as her husband for what happened to me, and in my darkest moments, I thought about going to the woman's house and strangling the life out of her.

But thanks to a firm push from my former Training Officer, Charlie Oak, and meeting Emma at a support group, I got my act together, but still feel guilty to this day that I even considered taking revenge on an alcoholic woman who was in an abusive marriage.

My ongoing rumination about avenge and revenge is the direct result of the death of a man who didn't deserve to die and nearly losing an important person in my life, a man who has become like a father to me, who took a chance on me when I was down and out, and let me work as an Investigator like I always dreamed about doing.

Revenge may be a dish best served cold but it sure burns up a lot of lives around it.

Chapter One - Present

Barry Sterne was staring at himself in the bathroom mirror, brushing his teeth, and wondering if he would stop aging so fast now that he was out of prison.

Barry was forty five years old when he was sent to Millhaven Institution, near Kingston in eastern Ontario, and prior to that, before he lost all of his friends, many told him he looked half his age. He had dark brown, very curly hair, not a speck of gray, bright green eyes, a smooth complexion with no wrinkles, and a perpetual five o'clock shadow, again not a speck of gray among his whiskers.

But now, seven years later, the mirror told Barry a completely different story, and he knew he looked a lot older than fifty two. The curls were long gone, he kept his hair in a short brush cut and it was mostly white, his eyes were rheumy, his skin had a sickly pallor, and wrinkles were trailing away from both sides of his mouth and his eyes. Definitely not laugh lines, he knew.

Old before my time, Barry thought, but prison will do that to you. When out of his cell for work duty or rec time, he would see other prisoners, mostly lifers, shuffling along the corridors, stooped over and shaky, and he would guess they had to be at least in their late seventies. But when, out of curiosity, he casually asked around, making sure he didn't draw attention to himself, he was surprised to find out most of those men were barely out of their fifties. Now, looking at himself in the mirror, Barry figured other prisoners must have thought the same thing about him.

Barry finished brushing his teeth and then got in the shower, noticing the large rust stain around the tub drain and the missing tiles on the walls. The bathroom was as shabby and out of date as the rest of his motel room, but after seven years in a small cell and sharing a shower area with other men, he wasn't about to complain.

After being released on parole, he was supposed to stay in a room at a transition house for several months and receive counselling as well as help from a social worker to find a job and a place to live on his own. But there was no space currently available at the only two transition houses in Brantford, so they put him in a room at a rather sketchy motel on Colborne Street East and gave him taxi vouchers so he could get to one of the houses for his counselling sessions.

After showering, thankfully there was actually lots of hot water, Barry dressed in jeans and a golf shirt and sat on the bed watching an early morning news program on the small flat screen TV sitting on the narrow, scarred desk up against the wall of his room.

It was just after 7 am, and Barry was unable to sleep any later because he was used to being woken up early in jail whether he wanted to get up or not, and he had a couple of hours to kill before calling for a taxi to take him to the transition house.

Being mid-July, the room was hot and stuffy, and even though the old air conditioning unit in the window was running, it didn't seem to be making much of a difference.

As he watched the morning show hosts bantering back and forth, Barry thought about his future, and what he was going to do to try and get his life back together.

Before going to jail, he was a successful CPA with his own practice and a good roster of clients, both individuals and businesses and was planning an expansion, adding at least two more chartered accountants. He had been fascinated with numbers since he was a kid growing up in Hamilton and started studying mathematics at McMaster University with the thought of working in research, but he was drawn to accounting; balance sheets, assets and deficits, depreciation, investments, and tax calculations. So he switched and got a degree in accounting then entered the CPA program, taking a job at a Stoney Creek firm to complete his practical hours.

During his last year at McMaster, Barry met his now ex-wife Rose at a pub night he attended with some friends, one of whom knew a couple of the girls sitting at the table beside them. Rose was very petite with a creamy complexion, freckles, and shoulder-length red hair, and Barry ended up sitting beside her when the people at the two tables decided to get together. Rose was a history major and had a different personality than Barry who, while not shy, did tend to be a bit of an introvert while Rose was quite gregarious with a sharp wit and an easy laugh.

Barry always thought Rose was well named because she had the hair and complexion of the flower, as well as the barbs. But opposites often attract and that was the case with Barry and Rose who hooked up that pub night and by the final semester they were living together in an off-campus apartment.

Rose's mother wanted a big fancy affair but they decided to get married in a civil ceremony at Hamilton City Hall. Rose got pregnant right away and gave birth to a daughter they named Hanna. They both wanted more children, but Rose had some serious complications during Hanna's delivery and her specialist warned that another pregnancy would be very medically risky.

Rose was from Brantford, a city of approximately one hundred thousand residents located about half an hour west of Hamilton. Her father, Jackson Andrews, owned a successful warehouse and distribution company and was one of the first to build a facility in the new business district off Highway 403, just west of the city. Andrews was a very wealthy man and Barry knew that Rose had never wanted for anything. Barry used to tease her by saying, "You're supposed to be a rose but you're obviously the apple of your father's eye."

Once he got his CPA, Barry was hoping to start his own accounting firm in Hamilton, but Rose's father started pitching the idea of them moving to Brantford. Andrews said Barry could have all of his company's accounting work as a base client to start his own firm, but it had to be based in Brantford. It was obvious to Barry that the stipulation that he move to Brantford was Andrews way of having his daughter and his now three year old granddaughter close by.

But, in 2003, Barry and Rose used a low-interest loan from her father, to be paid back by Barry's work for Rose's father's company, to buy a ranch-style home in north Brantford. And Barry leased a closed storefront on Market Street South in the city's downtown for his accounting firm.

It was a good time to move to Brantford. The city, once a thriving manufacturing center, fell on some bad economic times in the late 1980s and it continued for most of the 1990s. But by the time Barry moved there, Brantford was in a real rebound with new businesses being built along the Highway 403 corridor and a massive housing development in the west end. When Barry went to jail in 2016, Brantford was considered one of the fastest growing areas in Ontario.

Thanks to his father-in-law's contacts in the business community, Barry quickly built up a strong client base and within five years he had a full-time staff of five, including two other CPAs, and was earning a six-figure income. He bought a substantially larger home in an exclusive area of the Shellard Lane subdivision in west Brantford and he, Rose, and daughter Hanna wore designer clothing and enjoyed expensive vacations.

While all of this was fine, there was a problem that started as soon as Barry took over his father-in-law's business accounts and it got steadily worse as each year went by.

It became clear that Jackson Andrews' largesse in giving Barry his business's work had nothing to do with Andrews helping his daughter's husband get his firm started, but rather having someone he could use to cover up some shady accounting practices. Barry found himself dealing with doctored invoices, purchase orders for stock that didn't exist in the inventory, and payroll payments for employee overtime with no corresponding time sheets.

At first, Barry put all of the discrepancies down to poor record keeping and some incompetent inputting of data on-site and he expressed his concerns to his father-in-law, telling Andrews he needed to fix the problems at the warehouse, fire the on-site accountants and hire competent replacements.

"You fix it," Andrews said the first time Barry brought up his concerns.

"Jackson, these kinds of things can't be fixed at my end without illegally manipulating the audited statements," Barry told his father-in-law. "If Canada Revenue ever decided to do a full audit and caught the fact you were manipulating revenue and expenses to reduce your taxes and increase profit, you would be in very serious legal trouble, and not just you, me as well. I could go to jail."

"Nobody is going to jail, don't be dramatic," Andrews said emphatically. Jackson Andrews was a tall, thin man who carried himself with a kind of aristocratic bearing. He had a narrow face with a hawk-like nose and kept his thin, white hair short and swept back from his forehead. He always wore a dark, tailored suit with a white shirt and dark red or blue tie, like those favoured by American Presidents, something that Barry thought Andrews did on purpose.

"Rose tells me you're some kind of a genius with numbers and accounting," Andrews continued. "So, I'm sure, keeping my books presentable should be quite easy for you."

"Is there a problem with your business I should know about?" Barry asked, concerned about the way the conversation was going.

"Listen to me very closely," Andrews said with anger rising in his voice. They were holding their meeting in Barry's downtown office and Andrews, who was sitting on a chair facing Barry's desk, stood up and leaned across the top of the desk, his hands flat on the top of it and his face much closer to Barry's.

Andrews then said, "Thanks to my business as a start and all of the clients I'm sending your way, you're going to be very successful and earn a shit-load of money. You're going to build a very comfortable life for yourself, and more importantly, for my daughter and granddaughter. You'll have me to thank for that, not you, a meek bean counter from Hamilton, but me. And don't think for one second that I'm not prepared to take it all away."

Barry rolled his chair back from his desk to give himself some space from his father-in-law, whose face was twisted in anger, his eyes narrowed. Barry stood up, hoping it would make him look stronger, but he knew Andrews probably saw the fear in his eyes and his shaky hands.

"I could ruin you in this city just like that," Andrews said, snapping his fingers in Barry's face. "I pull my business and spread the word you're a fuck up and you'll be done in two months. Rose will leave you and come and live with her mother and me, and bring Hanna with her."

"I could take what I know to the authorities," Barry said, trying desperately to sound firm, but he was betrayed when his voice broke.

"Same result," Andrews scoffed. "I can afford the best lawyers money can buy, can you? They will ensure that you take all of the blame for not informing me about any accounting irregularities and you, my friend, will be the one going to jail."

Barry sat back down in his chair and stared at Andrews in disbelief. Andrews stood back erect from his position leaning over the desk. His expression softened as did his voice as he said, "Barry, listen to me. You're a good man and very smart. Just continue what you're doing and I will make sure you're well looked after. Okay?"

"Okay," Barry answered sheepishly.

So Barry continued to do his magic on his father-in-law's accounts, spending hours in front of his office computer manipulating numbers and even more hours at Andrews' distribution warehouse coordinating the on-site paperwork and data entry. He made sure he was the only one handling the Andrews account, hiring the two other CPAs to work with the other clients.

But the guilt Barry felt over what he was doing grew worse as time went on and it was taking its toll. He had a pit in his stomach that never went away, he slept poorly and was constantly exhausted, had no appetite, and started to hate the thought of going into the office and doing what he used to enjoy so much; working with numbers.

And it was having a serious impact on his marriage. While Barry adored and doted on his daughter, Hanna, he and Rose started fighting all the time.

While he once got a kick out of what he jokingly called Rose's 'thorny' side, he now found her constant chirping about some issue and her snide remarks irritating. For her part, Rose angrily complained about Barry's disinterest in her physically, his lack of energy and always avoiding attending family functions or going to dinner at her parent's.

There were many times during their heated arguments that Barry came close to telling Rose exactly why he was acting the way he was, informing her about what kind of man her father really was, and the illegal things he had to do every day for Jackson Andrews. But Barry couldn't bring himself to do it because he still cared about Rose and didn't want to hurt her and, in turn, hurt Hanna, who loved her grandpa. As well, Barry figured Rose wouldn't believe him anyway because she worshipped her father and took great pride in his social standing in the community.

Ten years went by and Jackson Andrews got richer, thanks to Barry's brilliant accounting work, and Barry's earnings climbed into the high six-figure range

But Barry didn't care, Rose did, but he didn't, because the money always had some guilt attached to it. He and Rose finally stopped fighting, not because they achieved some kind of compromise, but because they simply started staying out of each other's way. They lived in the same house, ate meals together, and put on a good parental show for Hanna, but otherwise, they barely interacted. They never discussed separation or divorce because neither one wanted Hanna to go through that.

Then Barry hired Farah Ahmed and for the first time in a decade, Barry felt the dark cloud around him fading away and he actually had a reason to be happy again.

But now, almost eight years later, Barry was sitting on the bed in a cheap motel, a convicted felon just out of prison who doubted anyone would ever let him near a balance sheet again.

Barry continued to mindlessly watch the television, sensing the start of a migraine, probably caused by stress. He told himself he needed to stop thinking about what happened, he did enough of that in his jail cell over the past seven years. He was considering getting up and taking an

Advil when there was a knock on the door. Barry hadn't called for a taxi yet so he couldn't guess who would be at his door early in the morning unless it was the motel Manager and there was a problem.

He opened the door and said to his visitor, "I didn't expect to see you."

CPA Barry Sterne saw the gun and then nothing else.

Chapter Two - 2016

"Good morning, Ladies and Gentlemen," Jason Burke said after standing up and walking from behind his table to the area right of the Judge's bench and facing the jury.

Jason was considered one of the best criminal defence lawyers in Ontario and could have easily had a successful practice in a major city, including Toronto, but he chose to remain in his hometown of Brantford.

Because of his involvement in previous high-profile trials that ended in acquittals, some members of the jury were aware of Jason's reputation, which he considered to be to his advantage. During jury selection, after the Crown Prosecutor had already used her twelve peremptory challenges, there were still some prospective jurors, when asked, who said they knew who Jason Burke was, but the Prosecutor had no choice but to let them sit for the trial.

Jason's appearance also made him easily recognizable. He stood well over six feet tall and was a big man, not obese, but big-boned, although he did have lots of extra weight thanks to his love of gourmet food. Jason had a dark complexion, he tried to keep a tan year-round because he thought it made him look healthy, sharp features and kept his silver hair combed straight back from his forehead.

Jason was an immaculate dresser, always in well-tailored suits, but for the trial, he was wearing the traditional clothing for lawyers appearing before the Ontario Superior Court of Justice; gray striped dress pants, white collared shirt, waistcoat, a long black robe, and white tabs, which looked like wings down the front of his robe.

The courtroom Jason was standing in was located in Brantford's Wellington Street courthouse, a two-storey brick and stone structure built in 1852 in the Greek revival style. Brantford also had a provincial courthouse located on Darling Street.

Jason often used a raised lectern at the defence table so he could keep track of his notes during closing and opening arguments, but today he chose to go without and, instead, stand directly facing the jury.

He looked around the jury box, making quick eye contact with each juror, and was comfortable with what he saw. The jury was evenly split by gender, six men and six women, although Jason would have preferred the majority were men since the victim was a woman. But they were all different ages and backgrounds, so consensus on a verdict might be difficult, which is good for the defendant.

After greeting the jurors, Jason continued, his deep baritone voice carrying throughout the courtroom.

"You've heard the Crown Prosecutor outline the evidence and testimony that she will be introducing to prove that my client, Barry Sterne, is guilty of second-degree murder. And according to my learned colleague, the case is simple and straightforward; in the early morning hours of July third, 2015, my client went to his mistress Farah Ahmed's house on Ninth Avenue in south Brantford and stabbed her to death while she was asleep in her bed."

"Ms. Ahmed was stabbed multiple times and according to the Prosecutor, it was a crime of passion carried out by a jilted lover who wanted to prevent the victim from spilling the beans to the authorities about his illegal accounting practices."

"You will hear from a forensic specialist that my client's DNA was found at the scene and from a witness, a neighbour of the victim, who will testify she saw my client's vehicle on the street the morning of the murder. The Prosecutor told you that my client had the motive, means, and opportunity to kill Ms. Ahmed. So it all does sound rather straightforward, right? Well, the truth is it's actually far from straightforward."

At this point, Jason hesitated and again looked at the faces of the jurors and saw, as he expected, acknowledgment of what he just told them. One of the things that made Jason a successful trial lawyer was his uncanny ability to read people's faces and get a real sense of what they were thinking. This was particularly handy when he was questioning witnesses and knew when they were lying.

It had been nearly a year since the murder, but at the time it occurred it had received a lot of public attention because there were few murders in Brantford, so the chances of finding jurors without at least some knowledge of the case were slim. As well, just prior to the start of the trial, there were several stories in the media recounting the details of the crime and providing background on the case against Barry Sterne. Social media platforms, including Facebook, had numerous postings from wannabe experts and internet trolls claiming Barry did it and a trial was unnecessary.

During the selection process, there were very few in the jury pool who didn't admit they were aware of at least some of the details of the crime. Jason considered applying for a change of venue because of all the publicity, but given the evidence stacked against Sterne, he didn't think it would make a difference to his planned defence strategy. In the end, even with his twelve peremptory challenges, Jason couldn't keep people with perhaps a preconceived notion of his client's guilt off of the jury.

Jason continued, "There's a lot of things the Crown Prosecutor didn't tell you during her opening remarks that you will need to know in order to make a decision in this case and I'm going to do everything I can to make sure that during this trial you hear all of those missing pieces."

"For example, the Crown will try and use the fact that my client's DNA was found at the crime scene as definitive proof he was responsible for the murder. It's a smoke and mirrors tactic, and I will ask you not to accept it as a fact, based on common sense. My client, Barry Sterne, was having an affair with Farah Ahmed, he openly admits that, so of course his DNA would be in Ms. Ahmed's bedroom. In fact, it would be much more suspicious if his DNA was not there, suggesting he erased his presence from the scene to cover up his involvement in the murder. But he didn't do that."

"You will also hear how things had soured between Barry Sterne and Ms. Ahmed because she was threatening to go to the authorities about the illegal things my client was doing with Jackson Andrews' business accounts. But you'll have to ask yourself why Ms. Ahmed would blow the whistle on something she could be implicated in and therefore put her own career in jeopardy. As well, you will hear Jackson Andrews testify that he somehow had no idea what was going on with the accounts of his own business and my client was solely responsible for the illegal accounting practices."

"And, finally, as this trial goes along, you'll realize that my client was not the only one with the motive, means, and opportunity to murder Ms. Ahmed."

"I'm sure you've all watched enough American crime shows on television to be familiar with the term, 'beyond a reasonable doubt' as the benchmark to reach a guilty verdict in a criminal trial. Well, that legal guideline is also a key part of criminal proceedings in this country. I can tell you that when the time comes for you to make your decision about the guilt or innocence of Barry Sterne, you'll find that the Crown did not prove beyond a reasonable doubt that my client was responsible for the death of Farah Ahmed. Thank you."

Jason Burke took a final glance at the faces of the jurors and returned to the defence table.

Chapter Three - Present

Shane Daniels was sitting in his black 1969 Dodge Charger in the parking lot of the Millhaven Institution thinking about one of baseball Hall of Fame catcher Yogi Berra's famous malapropisms, 'It's like deja vu all over again'.

Previously, Shane was in this same spot and was also trying to decide if he really wanted to walk into the prison and see a dying prisoner.

At that time, the prisoner was his Uncle Max Ivanov, who was serving a life sentence for the murder of his young wife, Alina. The terminally ill Max wanted to confess to Shane that he didn't kill Alina, but he did murder Shane's mother, and that Shane's father killed Alina. That confession set off a series of events that ended with Shane's discovery of his mother's body in a shallow grave and his father being sent to prison for murder.

Now, here he was back at Millhaven, only this time the terminally ill prisoner was his father, Ed Daniels, a man he once loved but now hated, and never wanted to see again.

When Shane was young, he and his father were very close and spent a lot of time together, in particular watching movies, including a lot of Westerns, his father's favourite genre. Hardly a day went by when either Shane or his father would come up with a movie trivia question to try and stump each other.

"Who was considered the pioneer of stop-start animation?"

"Ray Harryhausen."

"Who said, 'No rules in a knife fight'?"

"Actor Ted Cassidy to Paul Newman in Butch Cassidy and the Sundance Kid."

"Who said, 'Oh, I gotta helmet' before putting on a football helmet to ride on the back of a motorcycle?"

"Jack Nicholson in Easy Rider."

"What two famous singers appeared with John Wayne in Rio Bravo?"

"Dean Martin and Ricky Nelson."

Ed Daniels had a reputation as one of the best mechanics in Bruce County and worked out of his own repair shop in the south end of Paisley. He tried to teach Shane how to fix cars but Shane was not mechanically inclined and, instead, grew to over six feet tall and became a star basketball player in high school and later at Niagara University in Western New York state.

The Dodge Charger he was sitting in outside Millhaven was a gift from his father when Shane turned sixteen. It was a classic muscle car with a V8, 383 four-barrel engine under the hood, capable of producing 330 horsepower. His father refused to say exactly where he got the car, other than claiming a little old lady had it stored under a tarp in the barn on her farm.

Shane's partner, Emma, has been after him for years to give up the car, calling it a high-speed death trap because a 1969 vehicle had few of the safety features, like airbags, that are now standard. But Shane steadfastly refused because he not only loved the car, it represented a much happier time in his life. Shane kept the car in pristine condition, both inside and out, and had rebuilt the engine several times as he continued to turn over the odometer.

Shane and his father were mostly opposites physically. While they both had dark hair and blue eyes, Shane was tall while his father was only five foot nine with a compact muscular build and a much paler complexion than his son who sported a perpetual five o'clock shadow. They did share some personality traits; a strong sense of loyalty, quick to smile but also a quick temper, something that got Shane in trouble on more than one occasion.

Since going to jail, Ed Daniels has tried several times to communicate with his son, sending letters and calling on Shane's landline telephone, but Shane has thrown the letters away unopened and refused to take the calls from Millhaven.

The call about his father dying of cancer came from the prison Chaplain, Father Mark Hennepin, and the first thing that went through trivia buff Shane's mind was that the priest had the same last name as the first European to see Niagara Falls. His mind probably did that because he really didn't want to take the call or hear what the priest had to say.

"I've been visiting your father on a fairly regular basis since his diagnosis and recently he has been asking me to call you and ask you to come and see him before he dies," Father Hennepin said on the phone.

"Did he tell you that I want nothing to do with him?" Shane asked. "He murdered a young woman I cared about and is responsible for my mother's murder."

"Yes, he said you were estranged," the priest replied.

"Estranged? That doesn't even come close to describing it," Shane responded.

"It's your decision. I promised your father that I would call," Hennepin stated in a flat voice that clearly signaled to Shane that the priest felt he had done his duty and was anxious to end the call.

"What are they doing for him?" Shane asked.

"Not much, I'm afraid," Hennepin answered. "I suggested to Mr. Daniels that he request a release on compassionate grounds, but he said no. Medical care leaves a lot to be desired in federal prisons and your father is very weak and in a lot of pain. He only receives ibuprofen and acetaminophen because prisoners are not given narcotics. I have requested that he be moved to a hospice so he can receive more effective pain management."

"I don't care, Father, he should suffer for what he's done," Shane said.

The priest didn't respond to Shane's comment and instead asked, "When your father passes away, do you wish to be notified? And will you have any plan for his remains?"

"I suppose you should let me know," Shane answered in a flat voice. "I'll probably just let the government bury him."

"As I said, these things are your decision," Hennepin responded and then before hanging up said, "Thanks for taking my call. Good luck to you Mr. Daniels."

The phone call sparked three days of emotional response from Shane, ranging from deep depression to anger, and put him on edge to the point where he had great difficulty functioning.

The first day, he didn't leave his east Brantford home at all, just moved from sitting at the kitchen table drinking coffee to sitting in his living room easy chair, the same thoughts rolling around his head. He knew this day was coming, but not so soon. He expected his father to die in prison because he was sentenced to life with no chance of parole for twenty five years and would be a very old man by the time that happened.

Shane had made his mind up a long time ago that his father no longer existed to him and had consistently rebuffed attempts by Ed Daniels to communicate with him. But now this, his father dying, and the mental wall that Shane had erected telling him that he didn't care about his parent anymore came crashing down. All the terrible things his father did and yet deep inside, Shane couldn't deny there was still love for the man who meant so much to him when he was young.

His partner, Emma, tried to help as Shane struggled with his emotions, but they mostly ended up arguing. But right from the start of their relationship, they had agreed to never go to bed angry, so no matter how heated things got as Shane and Emma talked about what he should do about his father, it ended when it was time to sleep. Besides, Shane knew he could never stay angry at such a beautiful woman, with her flawless fair complexion, short blonde hair, brown eyes, and trim athletic body.

Emma Carstairs knew a thing or two about depression and up and down emotions. She lost her left leg from the knee down when, as a member of the Canadian Armed Forces explosives removal unit, a landmine hidden underneath the one she was working on exploded. The aftermath was a tough period mentally for Emma as she adjusted to life with a prosthetic leg and a boyfriend who left her because he couldn't deal with it. Shane and Emma met at a support group and the attraction was immediate.

On the morning of the third day since the priest had called, over breakfast, Emma said, "Shane, you've been tearing yourself apart for two days now and I'm really worried about you. I don't mean to be harsh, but you can't keep going like this, you have to get on with your life and that means you either ignore your father like you have since he went to prison, or you admit that you have some unresolved issues with your father that can only be fixed by talking to him, and doing that before he dies."

Shane didn't say anything for a moment, just looked down at the coffee mug cupped in his hands.

"I don't know," he finally said softly.

"Yes you do," Emma continued. "You need to look your father in the face and tell him you hate him, or you still love him, or you forgive him, or you can never forgive him. It doesn't matter as long as you take the opportunity to tell him something before it's too late and you spend the rest of your life regretting you didn't do it."

Emma reached across the table, put her hands over Shane's, and said, "Shane, I'm telling you this because I love you, but I don't want your father coming between us."

As soon as he finished his coffee, Shane called the prison to make arrangements to see his father and the next day made the three and a half hour drive to Millhaven, located near the village of Bath, just north of Lake Ontario, and about half an hour from the city of Kingston.

Millhaven Institution was an imposing facility, originally built in 1971 to replace the old, infamous Kingston Penitentiary and housed over four hundred inmates in direct observation units that radiated out from a central control post. There are observation towers at the corners of the facility, which is surrounded by a thirty foot fence topped with razor wire.

After taking several deep breaths to try and calm his nerves, Shane left the Charger and reported to the prison's security desk, showed his photo ID, took the walkway to the main building, passed through a metal detector, and was searched.

Because of his father's situation, he had been moved out of the general population to a separate area where he had a much larger cell to himself and Shane would be permitted to visit with him there.

Shane was escorted by a Corrections Officer to the cell where Ed Daniels was sitting on the edge of his narrow bed and he was shocked by what he saw. It was as if his father had shrunken; his once powerful physique from long hours of repairing vehicles was gone, replaced with the very thin arms and legs of a man deep in his nineties, not sixty eight years old. His cheeks were sunken, there were dark circles under his eyes, and his once dark hair was mostly gray and cut close to his scalp.

"So, Father Hennepin called you like I asked him to," Ed said, his voice weak and phlegmy.

"He did," Shane said simply as he sat on a plastic molded chair facing the bed where his father sat.

"You look good, son," Ed said.

"I'm afraid I can't say the same for you," Shane replied.

Shane's stomach was in knots, he felt some sweat at his hairline, and he was even more nervous than he thought he would be, his mind racing with thoughts on how this conversation was going to go.

"Yea, well, stage four liver cancer will do that to you," Ed said in answer to Shane's statement.

"What does the doctor say?" Shane asked, not sure what else to say.

"The cancer has metastasized and spread to my lymph nodes, so there's nothing that can be done. I don't have long," Ed replied, looking intently at his son. "Thanks to Father Hennepin's efforts, I was moved to this area and I now get a daily dose of morphine for the pain. I was told I was going to be moved to a hospice, but I don't know when."

Shane didn't respond and there was silence between the two men as they sat looking at each other.

"I'm glad you came, son, thank you," Ed finally said.

"I almost didn't and I'm not sure that I really want to be here," Shane said.

"Son, I know you hate me for what I did and I don't blame you," Ed said. "I hate myself and not a day goes by in here where I don't feel guilt and remorse. I'm not making an excuse for what I did, but I let my anger and jealousy about your mother get the better of me. I loved your mother so much, but all she wanted was other men."

"My mother!…" Shane started angrily, but his father put up his hands and interrupted.

"I know, Shane, she didn't deserve to die!" Ed exclaimed. "I know you loved her and she loved you very much," he said quickly, aware that Shane was now upset and want to say something.

"Again, I'm not making an excuse, but once I found out that Max Ivanov was my brother, we became close and I let myself fall under his influence," Ed continued. "When your mother said she would take half of everything if we divorced, Max convinced me there was only one way to prevent that."

"And you, a weak-willed son of a bitch and not the strong, decisive man I thought you were, agreed with Max that my mother had to die, without stopping to think about how it would affect the son you say you love," Shane said with contempt in his voice.

"Max just went ahead and did it!" Ed said, his weak voice straining to emphasize his words. "And then I had no choice but to tell you that your mother had left us and wanted no further contact. I didn't realize how badly it would affect you and it broke my heart to lie to you. I'm so sorry."

"Sorry? You're sorry!" Shane exclaimed. "I don't believe a word you're telling me. You claim it broke your heart to lie to me and yet you had no problem having Max hire a woman to forge a letter I thought was from my mother. That's not the act of a sorry, heartbroken man, it's the work of someone callous and selfish."

Shane's father didn't say anything, just sat on the edge of his bed with his bony hands on his lap and looked at his son with his red-rimmed eyes. It was at that moment that Shane realized why his father wanted so badly to see him before he died.

This was Ed Daniels' final act of contrition, perhaps suggested by Father Hennepin, and, as well, his father realized there were too many things left unsaid between the two of them. He knew that no matter what he said to Shane today, his son would be angry and upset, and would have a lot to get off his chest. It didn't fundamentally change how Shane felt about his father, but he did respect the fact that his father was allowing him to say the things he needed to say so he could finally close that chapter of his life.

Shane then asked, "Why, why, why did you have to kill Alina? She was such a beautiful, innocent person, who married Max to escape her tough life in Russia."

"I know you had feelings for Alina, but Max was convinced she was having sex with you and perhaps other young men in town," Ed replied. "He reminded me of what he had done for me and demanded I reciprocate. I had no choice, he had me over a barrel."

"Bullshit! Of course, you had a choice," Shane responded. "It had been years since Max murdered my mother, plenty of time for you to break away from his influence and do the right thing; say 'no' and own up to the authorities to what you and he did. But you didn't do that because it turned out you were just like your brother, a sick fuck who didn't care about anyone else but yourself."

"I deserve everything you've said, Shane, and it was important to me that you got the chance to say it," Ed responded and then added, "And I would never ask for your forgiveness, but please always remember that I'm very proud of you and I love you."

There was another long silence between the two men sitting in the cell and Shane fought an internal battle over his emotions; hate, revulsion, anger, disappointment, and even love. Why did this dying man sitting across from me, who once meant so much to me, have to ruin everything by doing what he did?

"I have to go," Shane finally said, breaking the silence. He was exhausted from the emotional roller-coaster he had just gone through.

"Thanks again for coming, son," his father said.

Shane didn't respond, got up from his chair, and walked to the door of the cell to signal the Corrections Officer who had been standing nearby.

"Shane, could I ask at least one favour?" his father asked.

Shane turned from the cell door, looked at his father for a few moments, then asked, "What?"

"I still have some money available to me to pay for it, but when I die, I would like to be buried in Paisley," Ed said.

"Okay, I will make sure that happens," Shane said, but then added, "But understand this, Dad. I will bury you in Paisley but it will be nowhere near my mother's grave."

"I understand," his father said.

Shane then walked away with the Corrections Officer, ignoring the tears welling in his eyes, knowing he would never see his father again.

Chapter Four - 2016

"I'm finished with this witness, your Honour," Crown Prosecutor Shannon Renwick said, then turned to Jason Burke, nodded, and sat down at her table.

"The witness is yours, Mr. Burke, if you wish," Judge Vernon Paget said.

The trial of Barry Sterne was well into its second day and despite his best efforts during cross examinations, Jason knew the cards were stacked up against his client.

He could see it in the jurors' eyes as they took in the testimony of the investigating Brantford Police officers who said the accused had no alibi for the time of the murder of Farah Ahmed because he couldn't prove his whereabouts. They also had a witness who saw Sterne's car on the victim's street around the time of the murder, and neighbours who heard loud arguments between the accused and the victim in the days leading up to Ms. Ahmed's death.

The jurors also listened intently, and several took notes, during the testimony yesterday about the forensic evidence collected at the scene. The forensic expert, Sgt. Royce Howell, led by Renwick, went to great lengths to repeat that no DNA evidence from anyone other than the accused was found in the bedroom where Ms. Ahmed was stabbed. Howell even went as far as invoking Locard's Principle that all perpetrators of a crime leave something of themselves behind, such as hair or fibre, but no evidence of anyone else being in the bedroom, other than the accused was found. The statement was pure theatre, obviously orchestrated by the prosecutor, and Jason acted quickly to try and discredit it.

"Sargent Howell, is it your testimony today that in the history of forensics, no perpetrator has been able to get in and out of a crime scene without leaving trace evidence behind?" Jason asked during cross examination.

"I didn't say that," Howell answered. "I just said that we found no evidence anyone other than the accused was in the bedroom."

"No you didn't, Sargent. Didn't you deliberately try and mislead the jury by mentioning Locard's Principle, something they might have heard about on television or read in a crime novel?"

"Your Honour," Renwick said as she stood up. "My colleague is trying to discredit the witness without foundation."

Shannon Renwick was a trim, middle-aged woman who had been a Crown Prosecutor for ten years and had a successful record of convictions.

"Your witness opened the door to the topic during your questioning, so I'm going to allow it," the judge ruled.

Judge Vernon Paget had been on the bench for over twenty five years and was considered pro-prosecution, so his ruling surprised Jason. The

Judge, who seldom changed the stoic look on his face, had a noticeably pale complexion, very white hair, and a neatly trimmed goatee.

"Thank you, your Honour," Jason continued. "Sargent, wouldn't you agree that finding evidence my client was in the victim's bedroom makes sense since he was having an affair with her?"

"Yes, I would agree with that," Sgt. Howell answered.

Jason then said, "I'm sure you and your team were very thorough, but wouldn't you also agree that even accepting Locard's Principal, it's more than possible that someone else, using precautions, was in the victim's bedroom and you simply didn't find any evidence they were there."

Howell hesitated and before he started to answer, Jason jumped in and said, "A simple 'yes' or 'no' will do, Sargent."

"Yes," Howell said.

"Thank you. I'm finished with this witness, your Honour," Jason said.

That was yesterday and today, just now, the Prosecutor had completed questioning Edith McIntosh, the elderly widow who lived across the street and two houses up from Farah Ahmed.

McIntosh testified she saw Barry Sterne's car on her street around the time of the murder, driving way too fast, in her opinion, as if he was trying to get away. Jason objected to the inference and the Judge gently admonished the elderly witness, telling her to just stick to the facts. He then instructed the jury to ignore the comment, as if that would do any good, Jason thought.

After standing up and moving to the front of his table, Jason said, "Good morning, Mrs. McIntosh. I must first compliment you on how, at ninety two years of age, you are still able to live in your own home and look after yourself."

"I still get around okay and my brain hasn't gone to mush yet, sir," Edith said in a smug voice, eliciting chuckles from people sitting on the courtroom's visitor's benches and from members of the jury.

Edith was a tiny woman, rail thin, and it was obvious she cared about her appearance; her heavily wrinkled face was almost pure white with makeup powder, her lipstick was bright red, and she was wearing a nice dark purple dress

"I'm glad to hear that," Jason said with a smile. "I see you wear glasses. How's your eyesight?"

"I had cataract surgery a couple of years ago, but don't you worry, I can see just fine," Edith answered, again in a smug voice and again earning an amused reaction from people in the courtroom.

Jason realized he was going to have to be very careful trying to punch holes in this feisty senior's eyewitness account because the jurors were obviously starting to like her and he didn't want to come across as a bully.

"Mrs. McIntosh, you testified you knew the exact time you saw what you thought was Mr. Sterne's car because you let your dog out at the same time every day," Jason said. "And you said you knew the exact date because you had a hair appointment that day. How many times a month do you go to the hairdresser?"

"I have a standing appointment every three weeks to get my hair done," Edith answered.

"That means two appointments could fall within the same month," Jason stated and then asked, "That could easily have been the case during the month the murder occurred, so how do you know you didn't get the two dates mixed up?"

"I'm pretty sure I got it right," Edith answered and Jason was encouraged to see that the smug expression on McIntosh's face was finally gone, replaced by what he hoped the jurors would see as a look of confusion.

"Mrs. McIntosh, you told the police and then the Prosecutor today that you recognized my client's car on your street the morning of the murder. I assume you had seen it many times before?" Jason asked.

"Yes, a silver BMW, hard to miss," Edith replied and then said, "My late husband was a car buff, always talking about them, so after fifty years of marriage I got to know cars pretty good too."

"No other BMWs going down your street?" Jason asked.

"Not that I recall, but his," Edith said and then pointed at Sterne, "But his was always stopping for a couple of hours at that woman's house, the one that got killed."

"When you saw the car on supposedly the day of the murder, did you see who was driving?" Jason asked.

"No, not from the angle I was standing," Edith answered.

"And you didn't see it parked at Ms. Ahmed's house, did you?" Jason asked.

"No, I just saw it driving past my house, going too fast, as I already said," Edith answered with some irritation and Jason could tell she was getting a little flustered.

"Just a couple more questions, Mrs. McIntosh, I appreciate your patience," Jason said with a smile as he continued to walk a fine line between getting what he wanted from the witness and not appearing to be bullying an elderly lady.

"Did you know the victim, Farah Ahmed?" Jason asked.

"No, never met her, Edith answered. "I would see her going in and out of her house, always wearing one of those headscarf things they wear."

"They? What do you mean by 'they'?" Jason asked.

"You know, foreign women. They always dress differently than we do," Edith answered in a tone that suggested she said something she thought everybody knew.

"And what did you think about my client being at a foreign woman's house on a regular basis?" Jason asked.

"Your Honour," Renwick interrupted as she quickly stood up. "Mrs. McIntosh is here to testify about what she saw and not what she thought about the people involved. There's no reason for my colleague to probe her opinions other than to try and put her in an unfavourable light for the jury. What she thinks has no bearing on what she saw."

"Your Honour, I would argue the opposite is true," Jason said. "It has been well established, and I can bring in a day's worth of expert testimony to confirm it, that eyewitness testimony is often both unreliable and prejudiced. If Mrs. McIntosh has a prejudice against what she called a 'foreign woman' living on her street and a middle-aged man visiting that woman, it could affect what she saw and when she saw it."

"Your Honour, this is not right!" Renwick said angrily. "Mr. Burke has managed to say in his argument what he was wrongly trying to get from this witness."

"I agree," Judge Paget said to the lawyers, then turned to the jury and said, "Ignore the comments made by Mr. Burke. They have no basis in fact and should not be used in any way in determining the credibility of the witness."

The Judge, with a deep scowl on his face, then turned to Jason and said, "This was a cheap trick, Mr. Burke, and you know it. I'll not have that kind of stuff in my courtroom. If you want to bring in experts to testify about the credibility of eyewitness testimony, that's your prerogative, but you will limit your questions of this witness to what she saw. Are we clear?"

"Yes, your Honour, I apologize," Jason said as contritely as he could.

Yes, it was a cheap trick on my part, Jason thought, but Mrs. McIntosh seeing Sterne's car on the day of the murder was a crucial part of the Crown's case and he had to do whatever he could to undermine it.

Jason returned his attention to Edith, who had a confused look on her face, no doubt wondering what all the fuss was about.

"Mrs. McIntosh, to sum up your testimony, would it be fair to say that you saw a BMW on your street that you had seen before, but you didn't see the driver and you don't know if it came from the victim's house. You say you remember the day because you had a hair appointment, but it's possible your hair appointment was on a different day in the same month. Is my summary about right?"

Edith didn't answer right away, obviously thinking about what she might be agreeing to, and then finally said, "I guess so. But I know what I saw."

"Thank you, Mrs. McIntosh. I'm finished with this witness, your Honour," Jason said and sat down at his table.

"Can I go home now?" Edith asked the Judge.

Chapter Five - Present

Shane was already in a bit of a foul mood and it didn't help any when he couldn't find a parking spot near the Burke and Associates office on King Street.

King connected two major one-way streets in downtown Brantford; Colborne Street running west and Dalhousie Street running east, so if you missed finding a parking spot, you had to turn down Dalhousie and travel until you hit another cross street, go to Colborne and turn left, go to King, turn left, and search again. Shane had to do this twice before he found a spot someone had just left.

There were a few parking spots behind the office building, but Jason had one and the others were assigned to the senior Associates. Jason kept promising him a spot, but Shane wasn't holding his breath for it and besides, in reality, Shane was out of the office more than he was in it.

After Shane parked the Charger and grabbed his cane off the passenger seat, he set the alarm he had installed, always worried someone would steal the classic car, and walked into the lobby of Burke and Associates. He was greeted by the receptionist, Jill Langly, the retirement-aged, matronly looking, woman considered indispensable by everyone in the office.

Shane had been out of the office for several days dealing with his father's situation, so Jill had a small pile of telephone messages and inter-office files for him.

"Jason wanted you to go see him as soon as you got in," Jill said and then added, "As well, Ben Chen called a few minutes ago. He wants you to call, said it was urgent."

"It's always urgent with Ben. Thanks, Jill," Shane said, taking his message slips and files and walking to his office.

Sitting behind his desk, Shane set down the materials Jill gave him and tried to concentrate on his plans for the day. It was difficult because he was still consumed with his visit with his father in prison, what was said between the two of them, and the fact his father would soon die. The range of emotions that Shane had been through over the past several days, anger and hate, sadness and remorse, had drained him emotionally, and he wasn't sure how long it was going to take for him to return to some kind of normalcy.

Emma had been his rock through all of this and he wasn't sure how he would have survived without her. She wanted him to stay home for a few more days and she would take some time off from her job at the Brantford General Hospital, but he refused, saying sitting around thinking about things would only make it worse.

Shane took a deep breath, told himself, 'Let's get at it', picked up the receiver of his office phone, and dialed Ben Chen's cellphone.

"This is Ben, the ninth fucking wonder of the world," Ben answered. Shane knew his friend could see his name on the call display.

Shane and Ben had been lifelong friends, they grew up together in Paisley, and they were an unlikely pair. Shane was tall and athletic, and outside of his occasional bursts of anger, was always careful and measured when he spoke.

Ben, on the other hand, was short and overweight, brash and loud, always said what he thought, and couldn't seem to complete a sentence without at least one swear word in it. But even with all of his bluster and self-deprecating humour, Ben was an incredibly loyal friend and would do anything for you.

Ben had been facing a trial for second-degree murder in the death of his elderly next door neighbour, but Shane found the real killer. The time he spent in jail until Shane cleared his name had a profound effect on Ben and even though he tried to cover it up by being his usual off-the-wall, potty-mouthed guy, Shane knew his friend went through periods of panic and depression.

Ben owned a popular Chinese buffet restaurant in Port Elgin, lived in his deceased parent's house in Paisley, and was very well off financially because of his side business as a video game designer. He used to love sitting at a table just inside the restaurant, overseeing the buffet and talking to the customers, often giving them a hard time as he enjoyed doing. But the murder charge against him, even though Ben was innocent, generated a lot of negative social media, so he often stayed away from the restaurant and let his Manager run it.

"I called to find out what happened with your father and see how you're doing," Ben said on the phone.

As part of his distressful process of deciding whether or not to go and see his father, Shane had talked to Ben to seek his input. Ben's advice was pretty simple: "Fuck him". But Shane decided to go and he now explained to Ben what happened and how rough the aftermath had been for him emotionally.

"I told you to forget that fuckwad, but what do I know?" Ben said. "But I'm now glad you went because you were able to clear the air with him and deal with the fucking demons he caused you. Now you say, 'fuck him', and move on."

"I'm going to try, Ben, but it's been a rough few days," Shane said. "Anyway, I'm back at work today, so that will be a distraction. I appreciate you calling and checking up on me, Ben. How're things going for you?"

"I think people think I'm fucking gay," Ben said. "And maybe they're right."

"You think you might be gay? Seriously?" Shane asked with amusement in his voice. "I'm almost afraid to ask, but why do you think that?"

"Well, I like wearing nice clothes, I run a restaurant, I live alone in my parent's house, I don't have a girlfriend, can't get a fucking date, and most of the time don't even feel like trying," Ben said.

"Well, leaving aside the so-wrong stereotypes you just used, are you even attracted to men?" Shane asked.

"I always thought you were kinda cute, and your limp and cane are kinda sexy," Ben said in a serious tone.

"You're not gay, Ben," Shane said, trying to match Ben's serious tone. "You can't get a date because you scare women off with your filthy language and weird opinions."

"Thanks for the big fucking pep talk, you're the best," Ben deadpanned.

"You're such a funny guy, Ben, thanks for cheering me up," Shane said sincerely.

"No worries. Maybe I'll have to get a date with something you blow up. Bye." Ben said and then hung up.

Shane hung up his desk phone and sat back in his chair with a smile on his face. What a guy, he thought, always coming up with something humorous about himself.

Ben was always there for him. When they were teens, he had shown up armed with a golf club to save Shane from a beating at the hands of three other teens. More recently, Ben saved Shane's life when he used the same golf club to stop a gunman who was going to shoot Shane as he was just about to go into his house. Shane was so happy he was able to at least try and return Ben's selfless acts by getting his friend clear of a murder charge.

Ben, who was overweight even when they were kids, dropped a lot of pounds while he was in jail, a combination of stress and the prison food Ben couldn't eat. Even though he loved food and hated exercise, Ben had managed to keep some of the weight off, which was good, but Shane was worried it was because his friend was still being impacted by the almost paralyzing fear he felt the entire time he was in the Elgin Middlesex Detention Centre in London.

Ben's 'I think I might be gay' routine most certainly lightened Shane's mood and put him in a better frame of mind to go and see Jason Burke, where he knew he would have to repeat what he just told Ben about seeing his father.

Jason had taken a real chance hiring Shane as his investigator because Shane was still dealing with an addiction to booze and pills resulting from the dull pain in his damaged knee that never went away. But Shane had proven himself to be very talented at handling insurance and pension fraud investigations, not to mention solving murder cases. He and Jason had grown close, no longer just boss and employee, and for Jason, the well-known criminal lawyer had become a father figure to him.

Shane knocked lightly on the door and entered Jason's spacious and well-appointed office where he was greeted by the lawyer with a smile and a gesture for him to sit in one of the plush guest chairs facing his desk.

Jason was aware of Shane's history with his father and was quick to agree when Shane had asked for some time off to deal with the situation. After they exchanged pleasantries, Shane filled Jason in on his trip to Millhaven where he found out that his father had late-stage liver cancer and didn't have long to live.

"And what about you, Shane, how are you holding up?" Jason said with concern in his voice.

"I'm alright, good in fact," Shane replied. "It was rough, emotionally, before and after I saw my father, but I've come to grips with it and I'm ready to move on."

"Are you sure? It's no problem if you need more time. Anything you and Emma need, you just have to ask," Jason said.

"I appreciate that, but no, I'm good to go if you need something," Shane responded.

"I do actually and it may be a complicated undertaking because it deals with something that happened more than eight years ago," Jason said. "I know you've been distracted, and rightly so, but I assume you heard about the murder that occurred two days ago at a motel on Colborne Street East?"

"I did. A guy who was just released from prison, shot when he answered the door," Shane replied. "Police have been pretty tight-lipped about it."

"And rightly so, given the possible motive for the shooting," Jason said. "The victim, Barry Sterne, was a client of mine. I defended him at his trial in 2016 on a charge of second-degree murder."

"That's why the name was familiar!" Shane exclaimed. "I remember the trial caused a lot of chatter around the city, with most people assuming he was guilty."

Jason reminded Shane that Sterne was accused of stabbing his mistress Farah Ahmed multiple times allegedly because she wanted to inform the authorities that Sterne had been falsifying the accounts for his father-in-law's business. Jason said he tried his best to sow seeds of doubt in the juror's minds, present reasonable doubt, and hint at other possible suspects. They found Sterne not guilty of second-degree murder, but they did find him guilty of manslaughter. Sterne was sentenced to the maximum sentence of ten years but given the chance of parole after seven, which he was granted earlier this week.

"Did he ever admit to killing the girlfriend?" Shane asked.

"No, he proclaimed his innocence right from the start and never wavered from that, even while in prison," Jason replied.

"I know as his defence attorney it wouldn't matter, but did you believe him?" Jason asked.

"I did believe him and I still do, and that's where you come in," Jason responded.

The lawyer told Shane that while many of his clients had claimed their innocence to him in the face of substantial evidence against them, he believed Sterne was sincere when he said he didn't kill Farah Ahmed. Sterne had told Jason that he and Farah were deeply in love and he planned to leave his wife so they could be together.

However, at the trial, neighbours testified about hearing loud arguments between Sterne and the victim, another neighbour said she saw Sterne's car on the street the morning of the murder, and a co-worker claimed that Farah told her she feared for her life because of things she knew about Sterne's accounting business.

"I tried to poke holes in all of the testimony, especially the co-worker, Eva Mendez, who I'm still convinced was lying about what Farah told her, but in the end the jury accepted the credibility of it all and convicted Sterne," Jason said.

"You said there were other viable suspects, so there was more than one?" Shane asked.

"Several to choose from, but they all provided police with alibis," Jason responded. "There was Sterne's wife, Rose, who claimed, unbelievably in my opinion, she had no idea her husband was having an affair. The victim, Farah, had managed to get a divorce from her husband, Amir, based on abuse allegations, but he's from a strict Muslim family so that didn't go over very well."

"And then there's the father-in-law, Jackson Andrews, who claimed he was unaware Sterne was manipulating his business accounts, again something I found hard to believe. Barry told me the illegal accounting was already taking place when he took over his father-in-law's books and he was forced into a position to keep it going. If Andrews found out Farah was about the spill the beans about what was going on, he had a clear motive to kill her, or have someone do it for him, and pin it on Barry."

"And Sterne had no alibi?" Shane asked.

"He said he was home alone at the time of the murder. His wife was staying at her parent's house, the state of their marriage is a whole other story, and their 17 year old daughter Hanna had spent the night at a friend's house," Jason said.

Shane then asked, "Was the neighbour correct when she said she saw Sterne's car on her street that morning?"

"Barry admitted to me that he drove over to Farah's that morning to tell her he was going to inform his wife that day that he wanted a divorce and to say he was going to go to the police and confess to the accounting fraud," Jason replied. "But he said he struggled to get up the nerve to do it, so he drove past Farah's house, turned around intending to stop, but couldn't do it, and drove home."

"What about the loud arguments the neighbours claimed they heard? Was that legitimate?" Jason asked.

"Barry told me their love for each other never faltered, but he and Farah did have some heated discussions about the accounting fraud," Jason answered. "Barry said Jackson Andrews had managed to isolate himself from what was going on, so if he came forward, Andrews would deny any knowledge and Barry would take the fall."

"I'm sure you did everything you could to keep Sterne out of jail. He couldn't have had a better lawyer," Jason said with conviction.

"I appreciate that, Shane, but this is the one case I've never gotten over and I'm still deeply bothered that I couldn't prevent a man I believe was innocent from being sent to prison," Jason said, some emotion evident in his voice.

Shane wondered if something was going on with Jason during the trial that, for some reason, he has chosen not to tell him about. It might explain the passion the often stoic Jason was showing as he talked about the trial. Shane decided not to ask, assuming that Jason would tell him if he thought it was important for him to know.

Jason then explained to Shane that after the verdict came down, he wanted to immediately file an appeal, but Barry refused. He was worried that if he ever received a new trial, he might be found guilty and sentenced to even more time in jail. But more importantly, Barry felt he had put his teenage daughter through enough and just wanted to serve his term and get on with his life.

Jason concluded by saying, "Even though he didn't kill Farah, I think, deep down, Barry believed he had to pay penance for his illegal accounting and for causing the death of the woman he loved."

"I assume you believe Sterne's murder is connected to the girlfriend's death eight years ago and you want me to look into that," Shane said.

"I do," Jason responded. "I kept in touch with Barry while he was in prison and when he was granted parole he called me and said he had decided he made a mistake when he wouldn't allow me to file an appeal at the end of this trial. He wanted to know if there was anything I could do to appeal his conviction and perhaps clear his name. I told him I could file a writ but even for a higher court to grant an appeal there would have to be some new evidence or a witness recanting their testimony."

Jason put a thick paper file in a manila folder and a flash drive in front of Shane, and then said, "That's were you come in."

Shane opened the file and while he glanced at some of the sheets inside, Jason continued, "My sources are telling me the police are already treating Barry's murder as an isolated event, perhaps a case of mistaken identity. "The motel he was staying at is known to be frequented by drug dealers and users, so police are putting forward the theory that a member of a rival gang shot Barry thinking it was someone else. The police obviously don't want to consider that they got the person responsible for Farah's death wrong."

"I'll have a look," Shane said.

"I still believe Eva Mendez, the supposed friend, is linked to whoever actually killed Farah," Jason stated. "I think she lied at the trial about what Farah told her and I did try to discredit her, but the Judge shut me down. His ruling was one of the grounds I felt I had for an appeal."

As Shane was leaving the office, Jason then said, "Shane, two things. If something happens regarding your father's situation, I want you to know you can drop everything and take care of it. And if Barry's release from prison triggered some kind of revenge or is an attempt to cover up the original murder, whoever is responsible may not be done, and looking into what happened to Farah Ahmed might be dangerous, so be careful."

"I will and don't worry about my father, that chapter of my life is now closed," Shane replied.

Shane spent the rest of the day in his office catching up on paperwork, he was responsible for background checks for the firm's lawyers, and reading through Jason's files on the Sterne case as well as the trial transcript. He wanted to collect as much background as he could on the various players involved and develop a strategy.

By 5 pm, Shane's eyes were burning and a headache was starting to set in from hours of reading and taking notes. He decided to pack it in for the day and was shutting down his computer when he heard a scream from the area at the back of the building. Shane left his office and quickly made his way to the security door leading to the small back parking lot. The door was open and two of the firm's lawyers, one of them on his cell phone, were kneeling beside a man lying on the pavement.

Amy, one of the legal assistants, her face red, tears streaming down her face, ran up to Shane and screamed, "Oh my God, Jason's been shot!"

Chapter Six - 2016

Jason never lacked self-confidence, but he had to admit to himself the Sterne trial was not going very well.

He knew this by reading the faces of the jurors and it told him, based on the look of boredom many had through huge chunks of the day, that the majority had already made up their minds that Barry was guilty.

Jason's efforts to poke holes in the testimony of the prosecution witnesses didn't appear to be raising any reasonable doubt and that was a serious concern.

The Prosecutor, Shannon Renwick, had just completed her questioning of Eva Mendez, a co-worker of Farah Ahmed's at Sterne's accounting firm and what she said was perhaps the most damaging testimony against Barry. Jason was hoping that with the background information he had gathered about Mendez, he could raise some serious questions about her credibility.

Jason stood up from the defence table and asked, "Ms. Mendez, you testified that Farah Ahmed told you she feared for her life because of what she knew about illegal accounting work going on at the firm. I assume you were concerned for your friend. Did you report what she told you to anyone?"

"No, I did not," Mendez replied. Eva was a middle-aged woman, of medium build, with a dark complexion, black hair pulled back and tied in a bun with some gray showing, and wearing stylish frame-less glasses.

"Why not?" Jason asked. "Someone saying they feared for their life is a serious situation."

"Farah asked me not to say anything to anyone and I didn't want to break her confidence," Mendez replied. "At the time she said it, I thought maybe she was being a bit dramatic, but obviously I was wrong and I've been heartsick about it."

"Did you know Farah to be dramatic sometimes? Exaggerating things?" Jason asked.

Mendez hesitated before answering and Jason suspected he knew why. She was probably worried that if she said yes and he found other co-workers to refute it, she would be caught in a lie.

"I can't say for sure," Mendez finally answered. "I just know that was the case at the time."

"You testified Ms. Ahmed had told you she was involved romantically with my client, so when she said she feared for her safety because of what she knew was going on at the firm, you had to have assumed she was talking about Mr. Sterne, and yet you didn't do anything about it," Jason stated.

"Like I said, I didn't want to betray her confidence," Mendez replied with a bit of defiance now in her voice.

Jason's years of experience reading the faces of witnesses told him this woman was not telling the truth. Why? What motivation would she have for making up a story that could play a key role in convicting Barry of murder? Was she just looking for some attention, spending some time in the limelight of a trial that has gripped the attention of the city? Or did someone put her up to up? For money, perhaps? Jason had someone look into Mendez but didn't find any red flags like an increase in her spending habits.

"Ms. Mendez, you testified that you were already working at my client's firm when Ms. Ahmed was hired and you became friends right away. Were you surprised that happened given your different backgrounds?" Jason asked.

"Perhaps a bit," Mendez answered. "Farah was from a Muslim family and Spanish was the first language in mine, but we both had marital problems and had that in common."

Jason left his position standing behind the defence table, walked into the area in front of the witness box, and said, "Well, Ms. Mendez, here's the thing. I had an associate speak to the other employees and not one of them was aware you and Ms. Ahmed were friends. In fact, they said you and Ms. Ahmed rarely interacted in the office other than the occasional greeting in the morning. How do you explain that?"

Again, Jason noted the slight hesitation before Mendez answered, obviously scrambling mentally to come up with an answer.

"We made a point of not fraternizing too much while at work," Mendez said.

"Ms. Mendez, I would suggest that you and Farah Ahmed were not friends at all and that for some reason you're here trying to implicate my client in her murder," Jason said firmly. "Care to tell us why?"

Renwick stood up quickly to interrupt. "Your Honour, my colleague is badgering this witness," she said. "But more importantly, he's using his questions to make statements about Ms. Mendez's credibility for the jury to hear that have no foundation and should not be allowed."

"I agree," Judge Paget ruled, and then looking directly at Jason, he said, "Mr. Burke, if you wish to refute Ms. Mendez's testimony, you can't simply use hearsay as a basis for your questions. You have to call witnesses to testify about the veracity of her statements. You'll have plenty of time to do that when you present your defence and then you can recall Ms. Mendez and ask your questions."

"Your Honour, Ms. Mendez's testimony about what Ms. Ahmed allegedly told her is being used by the Prosecutor as a key plank in her case against my client," Jason said. "For that reason, the defence should be allowed to aggressively challenge Ms. Mendez's testimony about what she was told by Ms. Ahmed."

"And you can, Mr. Burke, but not before you bring witnesses before this trial who will testify the relationship between the two women was not as Ms. Mendez says it was," Judge Paget said in a firm voice. "Until then, the jury must accept Ms. Mendez's testimony as truthful and you must stop asking questions that include statements based on third-party information."

"Yes, your Honour," Jason said and then added, "I have no further questions for this witness at this time, but reserve the right to recall her as part of our defence presentation."

"That is acceptable to the court," Judge Paget stated.

Jason sat down at the defence table and made a note to have one of his Associates start right away trying to convince the other employees at Barry's firm to take the stand and repeat what they told him about Mendez and Ahmed's non-relationship. All of them had been very reluctant to get involved, so it will be tough to get even one to come forward. But Jason had to try. He had hoped to discredit Mendez and perhaps break her down during his questioning today using what the other employees said, but the Judge shut him down.

The important thing was whether the jury, no matter what the Judge told them, would have suspicions about Eva Mendez.

Chapter Seven - Present

Shane walked down the long hallway of the surgical floor at the Brantford General Hospital looking for the family waiting room.

He had stayed at the office after Jason was taken away by ambulance to help deal with the situation in the aftermath of the shooting. Everyone was in shock and the Associates and members of the support staff were milling about the back parking lot not sure what to do other than stop momentarily to hug and console one another. As the firm's longest serving employee, receptionist Jill Langly was hit hard by what happened and just stood motionless at the doorway to the parking area, staring at the blood stain on the pavement.

There were at least five Brantford Police Service cruisers jammed into the area; one blocked the entrance to the small parking area, two blocked the entrances to the narrow laneway used to access the lot and two more were in front of the office on King Street. A forensics van was in the parking area and two officers wearing white Tyvek suits to protect against contaminating the scene were collecting samples and scouring the area looking for any evidence the shooter might have left behind.

There were two plainclothes detectives taking statements from the employees and Shane waited to speak to one of them, a man he had developed a professional relationship with, based on their mutual respect for each other's abilities. It also didn't hurt that Shane had saved Sgt. Mark Stabler's reputation by solving the murder of a wealthy businessman, a death Stabler was convinced was an accident.

Stabler finished talking to the shaken young law clerk who had found Jason laying in the parking lot, he signaled Jill to come and help her tearful fellow employee. The receptionist snapped out of her blank stare at the spot where Jason was found and started doing what she was so good at; taking charge of a situation. Jill put her arm around the young woman and led her back inside the office, telling other employees standing around to return to their offices and wait for the police to permit them to go home.

Stabler put his narrow notebook in the left inside pocket of his suit jacket and walked over to Shane. The veteran officer was a big man, tall, at well over six feet like Shane, but unlike Shane, he carried a lot of extra weight that showed around his mid-section, including a paunch that hung over the belt of his dress pants. He had a jowly face, clear green eyes behind a pair of dark-rimmed glasses, and short, very curly brown hair. Stabler had a gruff personality, but Shane liked him because he honestly cared about doing his job.

"I'm sorry this has happened, Shane, how're you holding up?" Stabler asked with genuine concern in his voice.

"I'm in shock like everyone else," Shane replied and then added, "But from what I overheard the EMS people saying, Jason was stable when they decided to move him, so I'm hoping that's a good sign that he's going to be okay."

"Did you see anything?" Stabler asked, taking his notebook back out of his jacket pocket.

"No, I didn't even hear the shot so I assume it was a small calibre gun," Shane answered. "I didn't know anything had happened until one of the employees screamed."

Stabler put his notebook away again and said, "Well, if you didn't see or hear anything, there's no need for you to hang around, you can go home, or you'll probably want to go to the hospital."

Shane looked at Stabler with a bit of a puzzled expression. "Yes, I want to get to the hospital as soon as possible," he said and then asked, "But aren't you going to ask me if I have any ideas on who might have shot Jason?"

"We'll get to that soon enough," Stabler replied. "We're just in the evidence gathering phase right now. I'll be back to talk further with you and the other employees about motives and possible suspects. I'm sure, considering some of the people Mr. Burke defends, that he has lots of enemies."

Shane saw that Stabler was now acting distracted, signaling he was finished with the conversation and wanted to get on to other things.

"I have a very specific idea about what this is about that I need to discuss with you as soon as possible," Shane said, trying to get Stabler's focus back on him.

"Fine, that's good, call me later," Stabler said as he turned and walked toward the other officers on the scene, but then he suddenly stopped, turned back to face Shane, and said, "You stay out of this, Shane, let me handle it. Don't get in the way. You have absolutely no authority to get involved in an active police investigation."

Shane didn't say anything, turned and started walking out of the parking area to make his way around the building and to the Charger parked on the street in front of the office. Not happening, Stabler, Shane said to himself.

Less than half an hour later, Shane had parked the Charger in the lot across Terrace Hill Street from the entrance to the Brantford General and had found the family waiting area on the surgical floor.

Emma was already there, dressed in surgical scrubs because she had just finished her shift in another department, and she was sitting beside Jason's wife Gillian on a short, well-used vinyl covered couch. The two women were holding hands and their red-rimmed eyes meant they had both been crying. They looked up when Shane walked in, Emma giving him a brief smile.

Shane sat down on the other side of Gillian and gave her a hug. Jason's wife, who everyone called Jilly, was what Shane considered a woman of elegance and class. She was taller than Jason and had thin, delicate features, green eyes, and stylish gray hair. Because she had been crying, Shane realized it was probably the first time he had seen Jilly when her makeup wasn't perfectly applied and her demeanor calm and composed.

While Jason concentrated his efforts on his work in the courtroom, Jilly was well known in the city for her philanthropy and for sitting on the Boards of several charitable organizations.

"How're you holding up, Jilly? What have you been told?" Shane asked.

"He was apparently unconscious when they brought him in, but his vital signs were good," Gillian answered. "He's currently in surgery, they think the bullet is lodged in his abdomen."

"He's going to be okay, I know it," Shane stated.

"I sure hope so, but the wait to find out is upsetting," Gillian responded.

"How about a coffee, Jilly?" Emma asked. "Shane and I will go get us some."

"I could use it and you could probably use a break from holding my hand," Gillian said, trying to put on a smile.

"I'll hold your hand all day if it helps," Emma responded as she got up from the couch. "We won't be long."

Shane knew Emma wanted to go with him so she could find out what he knew about the shooting. They waited at the elevator to go down to the first floor where they could get coffee from a Tim Horton's which was located inside the hospital.

"What's going on Shane? Who would hate Jason so much that they wanted to kill him?" Emma asked.

"I can't prove it yet, but I'm convinced it's connected to the murder earlier this week of one of Jason's former clients who was just released from prison on parole," Shane said. "It's just too big a coincidence to ignore."

"Is it someone looking for revenge for whatever Jason's former client did and decided to act now that he was out of prison? And then this person decided to act against Jason as well?" Emma asked.

The elevator door opened and they stepped inside. The car was empty, so Shane was comfortable answering Emma's questions.

"That's my theory," Shane said. "The parolee who was killed, Barry Sterne, went to prison seven years ago for manslaughter. I understand why whoever killed Sterne would have had to wait until he was released from prison before getting their revenge, but I'm not sure why they waited to shoot Jason. That's where the connection falls apart."

"Maybe not," Emma said. "Even though whoever did this could have tried to kill Jason at any time, they decided to wait until Sterne was out of jail and then take their revenge on both."

"You're right, that could easily be the case," Shane said.

"I remember the trial, as I'm sure you do, it was quite a big deal in the city," Emma said.

"I do," Shane replied and then said, "I met with Jason this morning and he told me he still believed Sterne was innocent and that he had never gotten over his inability to prove it. When he was found guilty, Sterne refused to let Jason file an appeal. Jason asked me to take another look at the case in light of Sterne's murder. I spent the day looking at the files and reading the trial transcript, and was just leaving the office when Jason was shot."

The elevator arrived at the hospital's main level, Shane and Emma exited, walked to the nearby Tim Horton's kiosk, bought three coffees, and returned to the elevator to ride back up to the surgical floor. The car was again empty, so Emma resumed their conversation.

"The cops are not going to appreciate you interfering with their investigation and you could get yourself in trouble," she said.

"I don't care, Emma, this is Jason we're talking about and I'm going to make sure the person who did this is caught," Shane responded with conviction. "Besides, while the police are looking for whoever killed Sterne and tried to kill Jason, I'm going to re-examine the murder of Farah Ahmed eight years ago. If I figure out who actually killed her, then I expect I will know who's responsible for these recent two shootings."

"Well, I know it goes without saying, but I'm going to say it anyway," Emma said. "If you start digging into the past, whoever is responsible for what just happened could target you, so you need to be careful. I mean it."

"I know and I will," Shane said.

After returning to the waiting room on the surgical floor, Shane and Emma sat with Gillian for another two hours before the surgeon, Dr. Jacob Anson, arrived with news about Jason. Dr. Anson was still in his surgical blues and operating room cap, his mask down off his face. Shane, Emma, and Gillian all stood up when the doctor approached them.

"Your husband came through surgery just fine, he's in recovery and all of his vital signs are good," Dr. Anson said. "A nurse will come and get you in twenty minutes or so and you can go and see him. I expect Mr. Burke to make a full recovery."

The relief on Gillian's face was evident, tears trickled down her cheeks, and she, Emma, and Shane exchanged hugs.

"How bad was his injury?" Shane asked.

"Mr. Burke must have been turning away from his attacker when he was shot," Dr. Anson responded. "The bullet entered the lower left side of his back and ricocheted off the top of his hip bone, losing its momentum and then lodging in his large intestine. We had to remove bone fragments from the area where the bullet hit the hip, but I don't expect there to be any problems with Mr. Burke's mobility. The bullet tumbled as it entered the large intestine, causing damage to a section about a foot long, which we had to remove. Luckily, it was not a high-powered round or the internal damage would have been too much to overcome."

"Thank you so much Doctor Anson," Gillian said emotionally.

"Your husband was very lucky, but it helped that his heart and lungs are in very good shape," Dr. Anson explained. "We'll have to monitor his recovery very closely for possible infection or scar tissue buildup, and it's possible he might need further surgery to do a bone graft on the small area at the top of his hip taken out by the bullet, but we'll wait and see."

"Thank you," Gillian repeated.

The doctor smiled, turned, and left the room, but Shane followed and said, "Excuse me, Doctor Anson, I had a quick question."

Dr. Anson stopped and turned to face Shane who asked, "Were you able to recover the bullet for the police?"

"What was left of it," Dr. Anson replied. "It was actually in three small fragments. As I said, Mr. Burke was lucky. I do a bit of target shooting myself, so I recognized it was a soft point bullet fired from a lower calibre weapon."

"Thanks," Shane said and watched as the doctor turned and walked down the hallway to the elevators.

If that slug is destroyed, there's no way police will be able to match it with the bullet that killed Barry Sterne, Shane realized. But hopefully, the police will realize there's a connection and, if not, Shane will need to convince them.

Chapter Eight - 2016

Barry Sterne spent over a year in the Elgin Middlesex Detention Centre in London while awaiting the start of his trial.

The Detention Centre, better known as EMDC, is a four hundred fifty bed facility, a large red brick building surrounded by high-security fences located off Exeter Road on London's east side.

Bail is rarely granted in a second-degree murder case, so Jason had to make the one hour drive from Brantford to meet with his client, which he did with increasing frequency in the months leading up to the trial.

They met in one of the small rooms set aside for attorney-client meetings, a windowless concrete box painted a drab industrial green with a metal table and chairs.

Jason was surprised at how well Barry had held up during his incarceration, a frightening experience for anyone except already hardened criminals. Aside from the so-called jailhouse pallor that was common among people spending any length of time in jail, Barry remained physically fit, perhaps adding a few pounds because of the prison diet, and appeared to be avoiding the anxiety and depression, also common with people who have never been in jail before. He told Jason he was keeping his mind occupied by accepting any work assignments that were available, reading, doing crosswords, and playing chess with other inmates. So far, he had avoided any conflict or confrontations with other prisoners.

Right from the start, Barry had proclaimed his innocence in Farah Ahmed's murder, saying he loved her and they were making plans for a future together. He admitted her discovery of his false accounting for his father-in-law's business and her pushing for him to get clear of it was causing friction between them, but it never altered how much they loved each other.

While gathering background, Jason asked Barry about his marriage and when he and Farah started their affair. Barry explained that he and his wife Rose's relationship started to deteriorate shortly after they moved to Brantford and he opened his accounting firm with Rose's father's business as his base client.

"Rose adored her father and he had always doted on her, so I should have realized that moving to Brantford was what they both wanted right from the start of our marriage," Barry said. "It didn't take long before Jackson Andrews, through Rose, had substantial influence over our lives and I didn't dare question or criticize what Jackson thought was best for us."

Barry told Jason the biggest irritation in his marriage was their disagreements over the parenting of their daughter, Hanna.

Rose and her father, especially Andrews, spoiled Hanna rotten and as a result, she seldom did what she was told, and hardly a day went by when Hanna wasn't pitching a tantrum, rolling on the floor kicking and screaming. The tantrums were usually the result of Barry trying to teach Hanna some discipline, Rose would get mad at him and let Hanna have her way. Most distressing to Barry was the fact that by the age of eight, Hanna was already overweight and both Rose and her father wouldn't listen to his pleas to stop feeding Hanna whatever she wanted because her weight would have an impact on the rest of her life.

"Because they wouldn't listen, by the time Hanna was thirteen and becoming very self-conscious, she was desperately trying to lose weight, trying every fad diet that came along," Barry said. "She blamed Rose and me, specifically me for some reason, even though I was the one who was always trying to get her mother and grandfather from giving in to her every whim."

"The other issue," Barry continued, "was that Hanna had some developmental issues, she was a bit slow, to be honest, but both Rose and her father refused to acknowledge that and when she was struggling in school, they disagreed every time I suggested we get her some help.

By the start of the trial, Hanna would be eighteen years old and Jason asked Barry if his daughter had been able to come and see him.

"At first, Rose, no doubt guided by her father, refused to bring Hanna to London to visit me," Barry said. "We talked on the phone, but Hanna said she wanted to see me in person and threatened to take the bus if her mom didn't drive her. Rose finally reluctantly agreed and drove Hanna to the jail. Rose waited in the car for her."

"It must have been tough having your daughter see you in prison," Jason commented.

"It was, but what made it worse was that Hanna just sat across from me and glared," Barry said. "I tried to get her to talk, to try and explain, but she just sat there and looked at me. She finally said that she wanted to come here in person to tell me that I had ruined her life and she hated me. Then she got up and left. It hurt me deeply because she means the world to me."

During one of their consultations at the EMDC, Jason asked Barry to tell him how his relationship with Farah Ahmed started.

Barry explained that by 2014, his firm had gotten very busy so he had been collecting resumes and doing interviews in order to hire another junior accountant, perhaps someone working on their CPA designation. Farah was one of the people he interviewed and he hired her that day. He thought she was incredibly beautiful with her olive complexion, fine features, dark brown eyes, and very nice figure.

"I was attracted to her, infatuated actually, right from day one," Barry said. "I knew it was wrong because I was married, but I had grown to hate going home at the end of the day and listening to Rose rant about one thing or another, something that, ironically, I loved about her when we first met."

Barry said that Farah was very smart with impressive accounting skills and it wasn't long before she was well immersed in some of the firm's more complex accounts. They started spending a lot of time together at the office under the guise of reviewing files, but actually spent most of it just talking and enjoying each other's company.

When she first started at Barry's firm, Farah wore a hijab every day, the traditional headscarf worn by many Muslim women, but after about three months, when she and Barry started to get close, she came to work without it. Her long, shiny black hair only increased Barry's infatuation with her.

"I didn't want to be disrespectful to her faith, but one day I got up the nerve to compliment her about her hair and asked about the hijab," Barry said. "She smiled at me and said it was part of being 'the new her'."

Farah told Barry her marriage was not an arranged one, but it might as well have been. Her family and her ex-husband Amir's family were close so they were basically matched when they were teenagers and it was expected they would get married.

"I liked Amir, he was a nice, good-looking guy," Farah had told Barry. "I agreed to marry him like everyone in my family wanted, but I also got them to agree, very reluctantly, to let me complete university first. I was always good with numbers, I even started doing my parent's income taxes, and wanted to pursue a career in accounting."

Farah said she and Amir got married a month after she got her degree and within a month after that he started pressuring her about starting a family.

"I was naive," Farah explained. "I should have realized how much Amir would be influenced by his traditional Muslim upbringing and his parent's wishes. Everyone just humoured me by allowing me to get my degree. I said I wanted to get a job, earn my CPA and have a career in accounting and Amir refused, backed by his parents and, hurtfully, by my own parents."

Farah said she went ahead and got a job anyway, doing the books for the owner of two convenience stores. The marriage lasted less than six months and Farah told Barry she heard Amir was already engaged to get married again.

"So, eventually your relationship became intimate," Jason said to Barry as they sat in the prison interview room.

"We were having a working lunch in my office one day and I decided I couldn't suppress my physical desire for her any longer," Barry said. "I just came out and told her I wanted to be with her and to my great delight she said she wanted the same thing. I started spending time at her place on a regular basis."

"Do you believe Rose when she says she didn't know anything about the affair?" Jason asked.

"I really don't know," Barry answered. "By the time Farah and I were seeing each other, Rose and I had basically no relationship, just going about our separate lives. She was spending a lot of time at her father's business and I told her I had to put in a lot of extra hours, which she didn't seem to care about, and she never questioned me about where I had been."

Barry said he was in his office when two Brantford Police Detectives arrived, told him Farah had been killed earlier that day, and asked him to go with them to the police station to discuss the situation.

"I was devastated, in shock," Barry said. "By the time I was in an interview room at the police station, I could hardly speak. It would have been obvious to the two officers in the room that I was more than just a boss upset about the death of an employee. Rightly or wrongly, I admitted to the officers that Farah and I were in an intimate relationship."

Jason could see tears welling in Barry's eyes, a clear sign that even after a year, his client was still dealing with Farah's death. A signal of innocence? Perhaps, Jason thought, or it could be shame and regret. Farah was stabbed multiple times making it appear to be a crime of passion and that's why Barry was the main suspect right from the start. But one could also argue it was a murder born out of anger and as far as Jason was concerned, that added several names to the list.

Jason looked very closely at Barry's face searching for any sign of deception and then said, "Barry, I know we've been over this many times and I apologize for that, but I have to ask one more time because your trial is fast approaching. Did you kill Farah? Because if you did, it's better that I know up front so I can mount the right kind of defence for you. The Crown doesn't have a murder weapon with your prints on it, but they have a substantial amount of circumstantial evidence that points to you."

"I didn't kill Farah, I loved her deeply," Barry answered in a firm voice. "I was prepared to accept the consequences of my illegal accounting practices, as she wanted, so I could continue to be with her."

"Then the question is who, Barry," Jason said. "Who knew about your affair? Who suspected Farah might go to the authorities about the Andrews' account? Who hated her enough to kill her in such a vicious way?"

Chapter Nine - Present

Shane wasn't sure what to expect when he entered Jason's room in the Intensive Care Unit at the Brantford General Hospital.

Gillian had called him at the office late in the morning the day after Jason's surgery to tell him that her husband was awake and was asking for him. Jason was in the office continuing his review of the Sterne file and trial transcript, and making notes on strategy.

The only light in the ICU room came from a soft fluorescent at the head of Jason's bed, which had been raised so that the lawyer was about three-quarters of the way to sitting up. The covers were up to his chest but his arms were free and Shane could see at least two tubes leading from the IV unit on his wrist to clear bags hanging from floor stands. Jason was also hooked up to several monitors on a unit beside his bed, measuring his vital signs.

Although he was a lot paler than normal, Shane did see a bit of colour in Jason's cheeks, which he thought was a good sign, and his boss gave him a weak smile as Shane approached. Gillian was sitting on a chair beside the bed and also smiled at Shane, a look of relief apparent on her face. Shane set his cane against the side of the bed, leaned over and hugged Gillian, smiled at Jason, and said, "What, you're not getting enough attention for your work in the courtroom so you go out and get yourself shot?"

"It would appear that way," Jason replied in a weak and raspy voice, the result of the intubation during his surgery.

"I was relieved to hear that other than a hip problem that might have to be dealt with, you're going to make a full recovery," Shane said and then asked, "How are you feeling?"

"I've got some pain, but whatever juice they're pumping into me is keeping a lot of it at bay," Jason said. "The only problem is it's making my brain very foggy and I'm having trouble keeping my eyes open."

"It's so you can get the rest you need and don't move around too much and maybe tear open your incision," Gillian said.

"I know, I know," Jason said in his sandpaper voice. "But you know I don't like not being in control."

"Oh, we all know that dear," Gillian said in a deadpan voice and then she and Shane laughed.

Jason tried to join in but ended up wincing instead.

Shane turned serious by saying, "I know you need to rest so I'm not staying long. Did you see who shot you?"

"Unfortunately, no," Jason rasped. "I was about to get into my car and I thought I heard someone talking behind me. I started to turn to see who it was and the next thing you know I'm on the ground in a lot of pain."

"Do you remember anything the person was saying before you were shot?" Shane asked.

"Not really, it's all rather fuzzy now," Jason replied. "I thought I heard, 'you bastard', or something like that but I'm not sure."

"Unless you've made a recent enemy I don't know about, this has to be connected to Barry Sterne's murder," Jason said.

"That's why I wanted to see you, to tell you that," Jason said. "It's too much of a coincidence not to be."

"I'm going to talk to the investigating officer and see if he's pursuing that angle, and I'm going to do what you asked, look into the murder of Farah Ahmed," Shane said.

"Thanks, Shane, but be careful. Sterne's release obviously stirred someone up," Jason said weakly and Shane knew the lawyer was running out of energy, so he said goodbye to Jason and Gillian and left.

Shane drove from the BGH to the Brantford Police Service headquarters on Elgin Street, a sprawling, single-storey, red brick facility that at one time he thought his career would be centered from. Being a police officer had been Shane's dream and he achieved it, only to have it cut short when a shotgun blast destroyed his left knee.

Shane parked, went to the reception desk, and asked for Sgt. Stabler. He had called earlier and set up an appointment. Stabler kept Shane waiting for half an hour, likely on purpose, before he got him from reception and took him to his small office off the open concept Detective's area.

"I never got a chance to congratulate you on your promotion," Shane said as he sat down on the chair facing Stabler's desk.

"Thanks, I think," Stabler responded and then added, "It's brought with it a lot more stress and a shit pile of paperwork."

When Shane first encountered Stabler, he was a Detective Constable and they clashed over the death of William Stanford, a wealthy Brantford businessman who died when he fell down the stairs in his home. Shane thought the death was suspicious, Stabler called it an accident, but Shane proved it was murder and found the person responsible. Shane kept his involvement low profile, deferring to Stabler when he solved the murder, so it ultimately helped the detective's career path.

Shane and Stabler made some small talk, Stabler asked how Jason was doing and then he got down to business by saying, "I agreed to meet with you as a courtesy. I know that Jason is both your boss and friend, and you'll be determined to be involved in finding who shot him, but that can't happen."

"Shane," Stabler continued, "You may work as an investigator with a law firm, and I admit you're a damn good one, but when it comes right down to it, you're still a private citizen. And just like every other private citizen, you're not allowed to be involved or receive detailed information about this, or any other police investigation. So you can push me all you want, but I won't divulge to you any details about what we know or don't know about Jason's shooting."

"Did you write all that down and practise saying it before I got here?" Shane deadpanned.

"Don't be a smart ass. You sound like that Chinese buddy of yours from up north," Stabler responded.

"Okay, fine, I understand all of that," Shane said. "But can you at least tell me if you're connecting Jason's shooting with the murder of Barry Sterne earlier in the week?"

"And why would we do that?" Stabler asked and Shane realized the Detective meant what he said about sharing no information.

"Because Jason defended Sterne at one of the most sensational trials in the city's history and there was a lot of public anger that Sterne got ten years and only had to serve seven," Shane replied. "When Sterne got out, someone got revenge, and then went after Jason for helping Sterne get such a short sentence."

"Not confirming one way or the other that we're pursuing that possibility. Besides, if someone wanted revenge on Jason, why didn't they do it after the trial seven years ago?" Stabler asked.

"Perhaps whoever shot Sterne decided they now had nothing to lose and extended their revenge to his lawyer," Shane responded.

"You know, Jason Burke is one of the best known trial lawyers in Ontario and has defended both the famous and the infamous," Stabler said. "There could be any number of people angry enough to try and kill him. As for Barry Sterne, there's a very real possibility his murder was a case of mistaken identity. There's a drug war going on between two rival gangs in the city and several top level members of one of those gangs were staying at that motel when Sterne was shot."

"My gut tells me differently," Shane stated.

"Well, I know from personal experience that your gut can't be ignored but, again, I can't confirm to you which angles we're following in both cases," Stabler said.

He then leaned forward on his chair, clasped his hands together on the top of the desk, and said, "If you really want to help, you can convince the people in your office to give us access to Jason's client files so we can compile a list of possible suspects."

"I'm sure they'll cooperate by reviewing the files and giving you some names, but you know as well as I do that you'll never get access to Jason's confidential client files without some kind of court order," Shane said.

"Just thought I would ask in case you wanted to help out," Stabler said.

"Don't try and put that on me," Shane said and then changed the subject by asking, "Can you at least tell me, as a professional courtesy, if a bullet was recovered at Sterne's murder?"

"Now you're pushing it," Stabler said then added, "But I will give you this one thing; Sterne was shot in the head and a slug was recovered by the coroner, but it was flattened because it bounced around Sterne's skull and can't be matched to any weapon we might find."

"The slug removed from Jason was also destroyed, suggesting they were both soft nose, low calibre bullets likely fired from a .22 pistol," Shane said.

"I don't know who told you about Jason because they shouldn't have," Stabler said. "It's not something anyone outside the investigation should know."

"Well, thanks for your time," Shane said as he stood up to leave, purposefully putting disappointment in his voice.

Stabler shrugged his shoulders and said, "I told you more than I should have, so be grateful. And another reminder, Shane, stay out of this and let me handle it."

Shane didn't reply, just grabbed his cane, put up his hand to indicate goodbye, and left the office.

Chapter Ten - Present

Shane drove from the Brantford Police Station to his office on King Street and was pleased to find there was a parking spot for the Charger in front of the building.

He stopped in the reception area and spoke with Jill Langly, who still looked upset over what happened, but had bravely come into work.

The office had been closed the day after the shooting while investigators completed their work in the parking area where Jason had been shot and had spoken with all of the employees who had been there at the time. It had been suggested the office remain closed to allow the Associates and staff time to deal with the shock, but several people, led by Jill, said Jason would want the work to continue.

Shane had a ton of phone and email messages waiting for him in his office, the majority from clients and acquaintances asking about Jason. He spend over an hour answering them all because he thought it was the right thing to do, but he provided only basic details about what happened, although he was asked a lot of questions by the curious.

Four of the messages were from the media, reporters for the Toronto Star, Toronto Sun, Canadian Press, and the CBC, not surprising given Jason's reputation. They called Shane because they had his name on file after he had appeared in earlier stories about some of the cases he had solved. When he returned each call, he was circumspect about what he said to the reporter, providing basic information, commenting that everyone was in shock, and saying police were still investigating the motive and who was responsible.

He had just completed dealing with the messages and had turned his attention to the Sterne file when Chioma Abiola entered his office and sat down.

Chioma was the firm's researcher and Shane considered her to be an invaluable resource for both information and advice. Chioma, a tall thin Black woman, had immigrated to Canada from Nigeria with her husband and two young children and was studying part-time to become a lawyer. Like Shane, Jason had taken a chance hiring Chioma so they were both grateful and loyal to him.

Chioma was off the day Jason was shot, but she had come to the office as soon as she heard, looking to see how she could help. Shane noted that she still had a look of worry and concern on her face and he understood because he felt the same way.

"What can I do to help?" Chioma said to Shane. "Anything, anything at all that you need, just ask."

"I do need your help, both for research and to bounce some ideas off," Shane replied.

He then explained that he had been told, in no uncertain terms, to stay out of the investigation into Jason's shooting. Shane told Chioma that was fine because he planned to look into the murder of Farah Ahmed eight years ago and he believed that whoever was responsible for her death was connected to the murder of Barry Sterne and Jason's shooting.

"So you're going to work under the assumption that Sterne was not responsible for Ahmed's murder even though he was convicted for it?" Chioma asked.

"Jason told me he believed Sterne was innocent, as he claimed, but couldn't overcome all of the circumstantial evidence pointing to Sterne as responsible," Shane replied. "I want to take another look, not necessarily to solve Ahmed's murder, but to see who emerges as the best possible person who would want revenge on Sterne and Jason. I need you to compile an updated background on the people involved; where are they now, what they're doing, everything you can find."

"Give me the file and I will start immediately," Chioma said enthusiastically, happy to be able to do something to help out.

"That's great, but before you start I could use your help in brainstorming theories about the murder," Shane said.

Shane had a large whiteboard on one of the walls in his office which he often used to write down ideas and theories about cases he was working on. He got up from his desk and used a cloth to wipe off what was currently written on the board in non-permanent marker.

Shane told Chioma that no murder weapon was ever found to link Sterne to Ahmed's murder and while his DNA was found at the scene,

Jason felt he had convinced the jury it would be suspicious if Sterne's DNA wasn't found considering he was in an intimate relationship with the victim.

"But there were four key things that pointed at Sterne," Shane said. He wrote them down on the whiteboard as he said them. "There was no sign of forced entry into Ahmed's house, a neighbour said she saw Sterne's car travelling fast away from the victim's house at the time of the murder, next door neighbours said they heard Sterne and Ahmed having loud arguments and, most damning of all, a co-worker testified that Ahmed told her that she feared for her life because of what she knew about illegal accounting practices at Sterne's firm."

"That was a lot for Jason to overcome in his defence strategy," Chioma commented.

"True," Shane responded. "But there's no question Jason's efforts put some doubts in the minds of the jurors, at least in terms of the nature of the killing."

"In total, the jury deliberated a total of twelve hours over two days before reaching a verdict. And based on the options outlined by the Judge in his charge to them, the jurors must have compromised to achieve a unanimous decision by finding Sterne not guilty of second-degree murder but guilty of manslaughter. It meant that Sterne would not go to prison for twenty five years before being eligible for parole, but got ten years and only served seven. In many ways, Jason probably saved Sterne's life."

"And there would have been people who were angry he only got ten years," Chioma said.

"There were lots of letters to the Editor and calls to radio talk shows condemning the verdict and the sentence," Shane said. "Farah's father, Hassan Gupta, was described in a newspaper article as being angry and bitter, and called the sentence an injustice. Even the ex-husband, Amir, lashed out, going as far as to suggest Farah had let herself be led astray by evil forces and she had paid the price."

"Nice guy," Chioma deadpanned.

"More about him in a moment," Shane said. "We should also note that Sterne's wife, Rose, publicly condemned her husband for what he'd done and repeated what she told the trial, that she was unaware of the affair. Interestingly, she also told reporters she was angry that her husband only got ten years punishment for killing his lover and ruining her and her daughter's lives. The daughter, Hanna, refused to comment on the trial."

"So, there are several people with the motive to kill Sterne because they believed he got out of prison too soon and to kill Jason because he made that possible," Chioma said.

Shane agreed and said he thought that Sgt. Stabler was being disingenuous when he suggested the Sterne and Burke shootings were not related and that perhaps Sterne was a case of mistaken identity.

Shane said Stabler was too good a cop not to be concentrating on a connection between the two shootings.

Shane had written his first set of notes on the left hand side of the whiteboard. Now he drew a vertical line down the middle of the board and wrote, 'Suspects/Ahmed Murder', at the top of the right hand blank area.

"These are in no particular order," Shane told Chioma and then wrote down, 'Rose Sterne'.

"Jason never believed that Rose didn't know about Barry's affair," Shane continued. "If she did, and even though their marriage was on the rocks, Rose might have been angry at Barry's betrayal and possible public embarrassment to her and their daughter. Farah was stabbed multiple times, suggesting a crime of passion, or perhaps in Roses's case, anger. Also, Rose would have had access to Barry's keys and if she knew about the affair, may have gone looking for a key she didn't recognize."

Next, Shane wrote 'Jackson Andrews' on the whiteboard and told Chioma that like his daughter Rose, Jason believed that Andrews had lied about what he did and didn't know.

"Andrews said he was unaware that Sterne was manipulating his company's accounts to improve its financial position and avoid taxes," Shane said.

"Andrews claimed Sterne was likely conspiring with company Managers, whom he had since fired, to share in the substantial incentive payments based on the company's performance. But Jason called Andrews a very controlling person over both his company and his family, in particular his daughter. He highly doubted Andrews didn't know what was going on, and was likely behind the whole accounting scheme."

"If Andrews found out that Farah knew what was going on, or even if he simply found out about the affair and was worried about pillow talk, he had the motive to kill her either himself or hire someone to do it," Chioma said.

"Exactly," Shane responded and then wrote the name 'Hanna Jones' on the list. He explained to Chioma that although everything he read indicated that Hanna loved her father, she shouldn't be ruled out as a suspect.

"She may have been just putting up a brave front for the public, but deep down resented her father for cheating on her mother," Shane said. "She was a teenager at the time of the murder, perhaps impressionable, and Barry told Jason her grandfather was heavily involved in her life and may have been whispering all kinds of things in her ear."

The next name added to the list was 'Amir Ahmed, Farah's ex-husband, who was known to have a temper and remained upset at the embarrassment he felt in the local Muslim community over the divorce. Farah was granted a divorce in civil court, but Amir refused to give his permission for a religious divorce under Islamic doctrine.

"But it appears that at the time of her murder, Farah didn't care anymore and was moving on with her life," Shane said. "She had stopped wearing her hijab and Barry said she no longer identified herself as Muslim."

"That would have just added to her ex-husband's anger," Chioma commented.

"And to her father's," Shane responded and then added, "But I won't put Hassan Gupta's name on the board because he was confirmed to be out of the country at the time of the murder."

Shane sat down and for a few moments, he and Chioma just looked at the notes on the whiteboard. Chioma, who always seemed to have a notebook with her, wrote down the information from the board.

"The problem is, to their credit, that even though Sterne was the main suspect right from the start, the police did do their due diligence and checked on each of the names on the board," Shane said. "Everyone apparently had a confirmed alibi for the time of the murder and Jason was unable to poke holes in any of them. But, I think that even though its been eight years, we should take another look with a fresh set of eyes."

"I can help with that," Chioma said.

"Check on the alibis and could you compile an up-to-date background on each of them to see if there've been any changes over the past seven years?" Shane asked.

"Done," Chioma answered simply.

"But aside from that, there's something I'd like you to prioritize," Shane said and then got up from his chair, walked back over to the whiteboard, wrote down the name 'Eva Mendez', and circled it twice.

"I need absolutely everything you can find on this woman," Shane said.

He explained that Mendez was a co-worker of Farah's and she told the trial that they had become close friends and shared each other's secrets. Mendez testified that Farah told her about her affair with Sterne and that Farah feared for her life because of what she knew about some of the accounting practices at the firm.

"Jason felt Mendez's testimony was the backbreaker at the trial," Shane told Chioma. "It demonstrated a clear motive for Sterne murdering Farah and Jason said he could tell by reading the faces of the jurors that they had accepted Mendez's testimony as creditable."

"Jason thought she was lying?" Chioma asked.

"He was convinced someone had put her up to it but couldn't prove it," Shane answered.

He explained that other employees had said, off the record, that they were unaware Mendez and Farah were friends, and never saw them even talking to each other very much. But every one of them refused to testify voluntarily to that fact and would deny what they said if they were given a subpoena.

"They must have been intimidated by someone who found out what they had told Jason," Chioma said.

"Jason believed it was Bruce Willard, the Office Manager," Shane said. "He now owns Sterne's firm, operating it under a different name. Jason called him to testify during the trial and tried to get him to admit he exerted pressure on employees not to cooperate, but without proof, Jason didn't get very far."

Shane then pointed to the name circled on the whiteboard and said, "But as far as I'm concerned, Eva Mendez is key. We find out who got her to lie and we'll know who actually murdered Farah Ahmed."

Chapter Eleven - 2016

There was no question in Jason's mind that Jackson Andrews had an air of importance about him, like a senior statesman, with his tall, thin build, silver hair, and expensive dark suit.

He also exuded arrogance, but it wasn't off-putting because you expected that from educated, successful men like Andrews, but Jason had no doubt Andrews used it to intimidate.

Jason got up from his chair at the defence table, shuffled some notes around, looked at Andrews in the witness box, and said, "Mr. Andrews, based on the testimony you just gave the Crown Prosecutor, we are expected to believe that you, a man said to always be in control, had no idea your business accounts were being manipulated for financial gain. Is that correct?"

"Yes," Andrews answered simply and said nothing else.

"Very embarrassing, I would think," Jason stated, hoping that by picking at the edges of Andrews' substantial ego he might get a revealing reaction.

"I had no reason to be embarrassed," Andrews kind of scoffed in response. "I did nothing wrong and was in shock that senior Managers at my company and my son-in-law had conspired to manipulate sales and inventory to improve their incentive payments. I took action immediately, firing the three Managers, and was in the process of dealing with my son-in-law when he was arrested because he killed his young lover."

"Your Honour, would you please instruct the witness to refrain from making unproven statements about my client?" Jason said to the Judge.

Judge Paget looked at Andrews and said, "Mr. Andrews, only answer specifically what you are asked."

Andrews didn't respond to the Judge's admonishment, he just looked at Jason with a smug look on his face.

"Mr. Andrews, I understand you've reached a settlement with Canada Revenue regarding the business taxes that were not reported and have paid a fine. Is that correct?" Jason asked.

"That's correct. I was in touch with the government to make things right as soon as I became aware of what was going on," Andrews replied.

"I also understand the accounting manipulation was brilliantly done, so much so that the government auditors could only confirm a portion of it," Jason said. "Your fine and back taxes were based on that portion. But Barry Sterne had been doing your books for thirteen years, so it would seem that you've made out like a bandit, thanks to something that was apparently going on right under your nose."

"Your Honour!" the Prosecutor, Shannon Renwick, exclaimed as she stood up. "Is my colleague making a speech full of accusatory innuendo about the witness or is he going to ask a question?"

Judge Paget scowled at Jason and said, "Mr. Burke, stop the rhetoric and only ask questions based on facts already before this trial."

"Yes, your Honour," Jason responded, looking at the Judge and trying not to get angry because he knew Judge Paget's ruling on the types of questions that could be asked during cross-examination was wrong. But the last thing he wanted was to antagonize Paget anymore than he already had. Jason then turned back to Andrews in the witness box.

"Mr. Andrews, you said you were aware there were problems in your daughter's marriage, but like what was going on at your company, you were unaware your son-in-law was having an affair. Is that correct?" Jason asked.

"First of all, I don't appreciate you connecting those two things," Andrews replied and for the first time, Jason noted a crack in the aristocratic veneer, revealing what Barry had told him about who Andrews actually was; a scheming, cut-throat businessman who would do anything to maintain his wealth and social position.

Andrews continued by saying, "To answer your question, yes, I was aware my daughter was going through a rough patch in her marriage and no, I didn't know about the affair."

"If you did know about the affair, I assume you would have been very concerned about my client sharing secrets with Ms. Ahmed and would have done something about it," Jason said.

"Your Honour!," Renwick said loudly before Andrews could respond.

"Mr. Burke, you have already been warned about the phrasing of your questions," Judge Paget said, raising his voice.

"I'm finished with this witness," Jason said in response and went and sat down at his table.

While the Judge was excusing Andrews, Barry leaned over and spoke close to Jason's ear. "He's so full of shit, everything he says is a lie," Barry hissed. "You've got to let me get on the stand and say what was really going on."

Jason turned to Barry and said, "The problem is, if you get on the stand the Prosecutor will question you extensively about everything that's been presented to the jury that points to you as the killer. Plus, you're the one who carried out the accounting fraud, so who do you think the jury will find more creditable, you or Jackson Andrews?"

Barry didn't answer, but Jason knew the debate over Barry testifying wasn't over. Jason had been saying no right from the start, but he knew if things didn't improve, there might not be any choice.

Chapter Twelve - Present

When Shane knocked on the door at Rose Sterne's big, two-storey home on a cul-de-sac in the north end of the city, a man answered the door.

He wasn't tall, but he had a gym-built body; muscular arms and chest straining against a t-shirt, narrow hips, and wide upper legs. His hair was cut close to his scalp, he had a five o'clock shadow and a deep tan.

"You must be Shane Daniels, I'm Bruce Willard," he said, holding out his hand to shake.

Interesting, Shane thought as he shook Willard's hand. Barry's former Office Manager, who took over his business is now living with Barry's wife. I wonder when that happened, Shane asked himself.

Willard led Shane into a spacious living room with a cathedral ceiling, dark leather furniture sitting on expensive woven rugs, and a large, low glass table in the middle. Rose Sterne was waiting for them, a beautiful woman as her photographs had shown, with her long, dark red hair and pale complexion.

"Mr. Daniels, I only agreed to meet with you out of respect for my late husband and out of concern for your boss, who I hope is recovering from what happened," Rose said as she indicated an armchair where Shane could sit.

"The doctors say Mr. Burke should make a full recovery, so we have our fingers crossed," Shane said as he sat down.

"So what can I do for you, Mr. Daniels?" Rose asked, already sounding a bit defensive to Shane.

"I was hoping we could speak alone," Shane said, glancing at Willard, who had settled on the leather couch beside Rose.

"Bruce and I have been together for five years now and we have no secrets between us," Rose said. "I will respect his advice on anything you're planning to ask."

"So, you and Mr. Willard were not together at the time of Farah Ahmed's death eight years ago?" Shane asked.

"Absolutely not! And I resent what you're implying," Rose responded coldly.

"I apologize, I'm not implying anything, just asking for clarification," Shane said, although, in reality, he was in fact implying Rose and Willard were an item at the same time Barry was seeing Farah. It would have made for an interesting dynamic during that time period.

"I assume you've already spoken with the police about your husband's murder?" Shane asked.

"I have and, of course, realized I would be the first person they would think of with a motive to kill my husband in revenge for what he did to my daughter and me by having an affair and then murdering his girlfriend," Rose answered. "But the truth is, by the time Barry was about to be released from prison, I had healed from the mental trauma I had suffered and had moved on. As well, I was already at my father's warehouse at the time Barry was shot and the police could easily verify that with the employees I was meeting with."

"I apologize, but I need to ask. How did your daughter feel about her father getting out of prison after only seven years?" Shane asked. "Did she still resent her father for what happened and has she ever expressed any anger at his lawyer for what happened at the trial?"

Rose sat up straighter on the couch, adopting a defensive pose, and said, "When the cops were here they asked the same thing and I told them Hanna was incapable of committing a violent act because it's not in her nature."

Shane noted that Rose didn't answer his question about how her daughter felt.

"Who do you think might have killed your husband and tried to kill his lawyer?" Shane asked.

"I have no idea," Rose responded and then added, "It's probably what the police are suggesting that Barry's murder was a case of mistaken identity and the lawyer was shot by a disgruntled client."

Shane decided to take one more poke at the bear before he left and said, "I guess it's kind of ironic that your alibi for the time of your husband's murder is exactly the same as the one you had when Farah Ahmed was killed."

"Again, I don't know what it is that you're implying," Rose responded sharply. "But if you will now excuse me, I have a very busy day ahead. Bruce will show you out."

With that said, Rose got up from the couch and left the room.

On the way to the door, Willard indicated Shane's cane and said, "I see you hurt your knee. I have a great personal trainer who could help rehab it back into shape."

"I'm afraid there's nothing left of my knee to rehab, I'm permanently disabled," Shane responded.

With Willard standing at the open door, Shane stopped on the walkway and thought if Rose's boyfriend was trying to be friendly by asking about his knee, it might be a good opening to ask some questions.

"So, you've taken over Barry's accounting firm," Shane said casually.

"I was his Office Manager and continued to run things until Barry was sentenced at the end of his trial," Willard said. "Barry was just going to close the doors, but I made an offer to buy him out and take over his clients, which he accepted."

"Barry had a very successful firm so it couldn't have been cheap. Did you have to put some investors together?" Shane asked, still trying to keep the conversation casual.

"Not really," Willard replied. "I worked something out with my bank and one of the biggest clients helped me out in order to keep a continuity of service."

"Let me guess, that would be Jackson Andrews," Shane said.

"And that really wouldn't be any of your business," Willard said and started to close the door, so Shane responded quickly.

"Well, this has worked out pretty well for you," Shane said. "Andrews sets you up in business and you move in with his wealthy daughter. Any chance it's because you knew about Barry's affair with Farah Ahmed and told Andrews about it, maybe suggesting to him that you thought Barry was telling Farah things he shouldn't?"

"Fuck off," Willard said and slammed the door closed.

Chapter Thirteen - Present

Hanna Jones lived in a wide, brick, ranch-style house on a large lot in an established subdivision in the Fairview Drive and Memorial Street area of north Brantford, her street lined with tall maple trees.

Shane had called ahead to see if she would meet with him, she agreed and was waiting for him at the front door when he pulled the Charger into her driveway. It was a beautiful day, with a clear blue sky, temperature in the low twenties, and a light breeze.

Hanna suggested they sit on the back patio and Shane followed her down a red brick walkway along the side of the house to a large backyard with a manicured lawn, wide flower beds around the perimeter bursting with colour, and a covered, concrete tile patio up against the back of the house. The patio featured an extensive set of expensive and comfortable looking outdoor furniture, as well as a round, glass-top table and a large wicker storage bin, currently open and full of kid's toys, several of them currently in use by a young boy sitting beside the bin.

Hanna was a big woman, carrying a lot of extra weight that strained against the ill-advised black spandex exercise shorts she was wearing, her large breasts were barely constrained by her pink halter top. She had beautiful blue eyes, full lips, a face covered in freckles, and like her mother Rose, red hair. But, unlike her mother, Hanna's hair was very curly.

Hanna introduced Shane to her husband, Corey, and her three-year-old son, Joshua, who was quietly playing with a toy dump truck. Shane thought Joshua looked big for his age, but he was a cute kid who had inherited his mother's red hair. The husband, Corey, was not much taller than his wife, maybe five foot eight, and was rail thin, the shorts and t-shirt he was wearing hung loosely on his body. He had long hair, tied in a ponytail, a pale complexion, and a thin moustache.

"I would shake your hand, but mine are a bit full at the moment," Corey said.

He was standing just inside the house holding one of the glass sliding doors for the entrance into the house off the patio.

"That stupid door hasn't been right since the day we moved into this house," Hanna said to Shane as they sat down on the thick cushioned chairs at the table. "It's always coming off the track at the top or popping out of the guide at the bottom. The spring rollers on the top need to be fixed or, better still, the whole door replaced."

Shane and Hanna watched as Corey tilted the top of the door forward, put it in the upper track, pushed up slightly, and set the door in the bottom guide. He slid it open and closed a couple of times to make sure it worked.

"Luckily, Corey is an expert at putting sliding glass doors in and out because he's had to do it so many times," Hanna said with a smile.

"Joshua, come inside with Daddy so Mommy can talk to her guest," Corey said to his son, who quietly obeyed, leaving his toy behind and walking into the house. His father followed him inside and closed the now operating sliding glass door.

"You'll have to excuse my husband, he's kind of shy and not much of a talker," Hanna said as she watched Corey and her son enter the house.

"No worries. He works at your grandfather's company?" Shane asked.

"That's where we met," Hanna answered. "I worked in the office one summer and Corey used to bring in paperwork from the warehouse for me to put in the computer system. We connected right away, but my grandfather wasn't happy because I was seventeen and Corey was twenty five, and he threatened to tell my mother and father. But he eventually changed his mind and said it was okay for us to see each other. I usually got my way with my grandfather. When we got married, grandfather paid for Corey to be trained as a tow motor driver and now he makes pretty good money."

"I'm sorry about your father," Shane said, changing the subject.

"Thanks. I'm still trying to deal with it and have been an emotional wreck," Hanna said and Shane saw that she had started gripping the armrests on her chair. She then added, "I was just about to get him back in my life full-time after eight years and now I've lost him forever."

"You and your father were always close?" Shane asked, hoping Hanna would talk about her family and perhaps give her perspective on the events surrounding the murder of Farah Ahmed.

Hanna explained that her relationship with her father was always complicated, primarily because he worked long hours and wasn't home a lot when she was young and when he and her mother fought, it was almost always about her. Hanna admitted that her mother gave her whatever she wanted and her grandfather spoiled her as well.

"And what I wanted the most, besides the best toys, phones, laptops, and clothes that money could buy, was food," Hanna said and then looking down at herself added, "And as you can see, I had no self-control and my mother indulged that."

Hanna said even when she reached the age when girls started to worry about body image and she tried to lose weight, it was a losing battle because she got little support from her mother. She often overheard her parents fighting over her weight, her father blaming her mother because she spoiled her.

"I did reach a point when I was trying to lose weight that I started to resent my mother for the way I was," Hanna told Shane. "My mother is a beautiful woman and I started to think she let me get fat so she wouldn't have any competition in the family and her social circles."

"It must have been very difficult for you when your father was arrested for killing the woman he was having an affair with," Shane said and then asked, "You were what, seventeen years old?"

"When I was told, I locked myself in my room for most of the day," Hanna said. "I went through it all; shock, anger, long crying sessions. I knew my parent's marriage had become a joke and I used to think I was to blame, but I never thought my father was the type to have an affair."

"Your mother said she didn't know about the affair until your father was arrested and in many ways that eliminated her as a possible suspect in Farah Ahmed's murder. Do you mind me asking if you believed her?" Shane said.

"To be honest, I didn't know what to think," Hanna replied. "By the time my father was arrested, he and my mom seemed to be married in name only, so I'm not sure if she even cared enough to know."

"Please don't get upset at this question," Shane said sincerely. "Do you think it's possible your mother, or perhaps your grandfather, would wait until your father was released from prison and then take their revenge for what happened by killing him and trying to kill his lawyer?"

Hanna hesitated before she answered and Shane wasn't sure if it was because she was thinking about her answer or really didn't want to say what she thought.

She then said, "Both my mother and my grandfather are known for their hair-trigger tempers, but they're not violent people. Their outbursts of anger have always been flashes in a pan, over quickly. I can't see either of them hanging on to their anger for over seven years until my father was released from prison. If they were going to do anything, it would have happened around the time my father was arrested."

"Could that perhaps have been the case if either of them did find out about Farah Ahmed?" Shane asked and then realized he had probably gone too far.

But Hanna didn't respond and the expression on her face didn't change.

Instead, she said, "Perhaps you should be asking if I thought my father was innocent. Maybe you should be asking if I actually knew about the affair and killed his lover, and maybe you should be asking if I was so angry at my father that I was willing to wait seven years until he got out of jail to kill him."

"If I did ask those questions, would all of the answers be 'no'?" Shane said.

"They would," Hanna replied. "The police officer who was here asked a lot of the same questions you have, but I got the impression he was going through the motions. The Detective, Sargent Stabler, said they believed my father was assassinated by a member of a drug gang who killed the wrong man and your boss was likely shot by the victim of one of his clients or one of their family members."

"Do you believe that?" Shane asked.

Hanna shrugged her shoulders and said, "I've lost my father, does it really matter who killed him?"

Shane wasn't sure if he believed all of the answers Hanna gave him today. If she found out about her father's affair, she could have been angry enough about the state of her parent's marriage to kill Farah, and angry enough to stab her multiple times. She lived at home at the time, so she would have had access to her father's keys, looking for one to let her into Farah's house so she didn't have to break in.

Shane and Hanna talked for a few more minutes, he thanked her for her time, walked back along the side of the house, and got in the Charger parked on the street. He was just about to pull away when he noticed the curtain in the front bay window open slightly and Corey sneaking a peak at him.

I wonder what he knows? Shane asked himself.

Chapter Fourteen - Present

The evening following Shane's visit with Hanna Jones, he and Emma shared a bowl of popcorn and watched the 2010 remake of 'True Grit' starring Jeff Bridges, Matt Damon, and Josh Brolin.

While he felt a lot of remakes failed to live up to the originals, Shane thought both the overall film and, specifically, Bridges' version of Marshal Rooster Cogburn were very good and stood nicely beside the 1969 version with John Wayne and Kim Darby.

Prior to coming home, Shane had stopped at the hospital to see Jason and found the lawyer to be quiet and withdrawn, not unexpected considering what he had been through and some of the pain he was still experiencing from the surgery to deal with the internal damage caused by the bullet.

But once they started talking, Shane realized that a lot of Jason's melancholy had nothing to do with his medical condition, but rather the late Barry Sterne and his 2016 murder trial.

"Since Barry was killed and I was shot, I now have all of this time on my hands and all I can think about is how I let him down at the trial," Jason said in a soft voice as he crunched on shaved ice from a cup to ease the dry mouth he was suffering as a result of the antibiotics and pain medicine being pumped into his body through the catheter inserted through the top of his right hand.

"I know that's not true," Shane responded forcefully. "I've studied the file and the trial transcript and I think you did the best you could considering the amount of circumstantial evidence that pointed at Sterne as the killer."

"Yea, well, I disagree," Jason replied. "I should have tried harder to put a defence together, found someone or something to try and refute what the prosecution witnesses were claiming."

Jason told Shane that Farah Ahmed had virtually no close friends, probably the result of being under the controlling thumb of her husband and both her parents and her father-in-law. That meant there was no one Jason could call to the stand to talk about Farah, perhaps her relationship with Barry, and maybe what she did and didn't know about what was going on at Barry's firm. That left only the testimony of Farah's co-worker Eva Mendez and Jason was convinced she was lying and maybe paid to do it.

"There was a conspiracy of silence and misdirection surrounding the entire case," Jason said. "And I think it was directed and paid for by Jackson Andrews in order to protect himself and maybe his daughter, Rose, out of fear she might have been responsible for Farah's murder."

"A good example of the conspiracy is the two Managers Andrews said he fired because of their involvement with Barry in manipulating the accounts to improve the bottom line," Jason continued.

"Those two guys, Randal Montgomery and Bill Wright fell on their swords for Andrews, who I believed knew all about what was going on. They said they kept Andrews in the dark. I wanted to put both of them on the stand and have them explain exactly how the accounts were fixed without Andrews knowing. But it was going to be a problem because they both hired lawyers who produced documents showing they had signed non-disclosure agreements when they were hired by Andrews and that they would fight any attempt to make them break the agreements. Of course, trying to hide behind an NDA is bullshit."

"But a side legal argument over what the two Managers could discuss on the stand would have dragged the trial out," Shane commented.

"It would have meant the jury sitting in their room, probably already impatient about how long the trial was taking them away from their jobs and family," Jason said. "They would be speculating about what was going on and I can tell you that my experience has shown that when jurors are sent out of the courtroom, they know it's because there's disagreement over something they should or shouldn't hear, and the majority believe its something bad about the accused. It's yet another seed planted in their minds about the accused's guilt."

"I met with Rose Sterne at her house two days ago and met with Bruce Willard, who's living with her," Shane said.

"The bodybuilder Accountant? He's a real piece of work. That's very interesting," Jason reacted.

"He was friendly enough to start, but when I asked him a few questions as I was leaving, he told me to get lost. Well, actually, he told me to fuck off," Shane said.

Jason said he believed Willard was a key figure in the cone of silence the major players in the case had built around themselves to ensure Barry was convicted of murder.

"He testified at the trial and I tried to challenge him on what he claimed he did and didn't know," Jason said. "But by that time, I had already made a serious strategic mistake."

Jason explained that with previous witnesses like Jackson Andrews and Eva Mendez, he had tried to inject comments about the truthfulness of their testimony to help put some reasonable doubt in the minds of the jurors. However, the Crown Prosecutor, Shannon Renwick was smart enough to call him on it and the Judge, Vernon Paget, no fool himself, shut him down.

"I wasn't subtle enough," Jason told Shane. "By the time Bruce Willard was on the stand, Renwick and Paget were listening very carefully to everything I said and asked, and I didn't have the latitude to attack Willard's claims. I tied my own hands and it's one of the things I deeply regret in my defence of Barry Sterne."

Although he seemed to have perked up a bit during his visit, Shane could see that Jason's dark mood had returned when Shane grabbed his cane and started to leave.

"I know the case is cold, but do you think there's anything you can come up with that might clear Barry's name from the Ahmed murder and perhaps solve his murder? Jason asked.

Shane stopped at the door of the hospital room and said to Jason, "I promise that I will give it my best effort. It's early yet and I have a lot of work to do, but something happened yesterday when I was interviewing Barry's daughter Hanna that's got me thinking in a completely different direction. But it hasn't come together yet in my head. I'll let you know."

Shane drove home from the hospital and before he and Emma watched the movie and munched popcorn, over dinner he filled his partner in on everything he had been up to during the past few days.

Shane felt that in addition to being a beautiful woman, Emma was one of the smartest people he knew and he often sought her insight on his cases. He knew that she was still worried about how he was dealing with the situation regarding his father and he thought that if he got her advice on what he was working on, she would see that he was okay, that he had moved on with his life, and didn't think about the man dying in a prison hospice in Kingston.

Of course, some of that wasn't really true; several times a day an image of the emaciated man sitting on the prison cell bed would enter Shane's thoughts and he would again, momentarily, suffer the conflicting emotions of love and hate. Why did it have to be this way, he would think, why couldn't I have had a normal family?

"You know, it seems to me you have more suspects that an old Agatha Christie movie," Emma said after Shane outlined the players in the Farah Ahmed and Barry Sterne murders, and the attempted murder of Jason.

"That's true," Shane agreed. "But the problem remains that everyone has alibis for both events, except for Barry Sterne during the time period when Farah was murdered. He admitted he had driven to her house around the time she was killed but didn't stop and drove to his home, which was empty because his wife and daughter had already left for the day."

"I know how Jason feels about Sterne's innocence, but isn't it possible this is a case where Occam's Razor applies," Emma said. "The simplest answer is the right answer. In this case, Sterne did, in fact, kill his mistress."

"I keep coming back to that idea myself," Shane responded. "However, Jason said he spent a lot of hours with Sterne, always watching for signs of deception and he said they were never there. He says Sterne always had great difficulty talking about Farah's death and his profound love for her was genuine. You and I both know that Jason has an incredible gift for reading people, so I have to trust him when he says he believes Sterne was innocent."

"I think you have to break someone's alibi," Emma suggested. "If, for example, there was someone whose alibi didn't stand up for the time

Sterne was shot and Jason wounded, maybe their alibi for the Ahmed murder is false too."

"I agree, but it's going to take a lot of legwork and I don't have the resources the police have," Shane said. "I keep thinking there's something in the original police file or the trial transcript that I missed."

"You'll get it, you always do," Emma said and then leaned over and kissed Shane.

"I sure hope so," Shane replied.

Chapter Fifteen - 2016

It didn't take much to realize that Bruce Willard was a bodybuilder as he sat in the witness box waiting for Jason to begin his cross-examination.

Willard had dressed casually but stylishly for court, an expensive looking sport coat over a designer polo shirt. His solid muscles were obvious and his shoulders and upper arms strained against the fabric of his coat. Willard's hair was in a brush cut, he had a small diamond stud in one ear lobe and his dark tan looked like it was enhanced by time under a lamp.

"Mr. Willard," Jason began, "You testified that you were unaware of the accounting fraud that was occurring with the Andrews' accounts. As the Office Manager, wasn't it your responsibility to monitor all of the accounts at my client's firm?"

"Yes, but as I told the Prosecutor, Barry handled the Andrews' account exclusively and no one else was allowed access to it," Willard replied.

"You didn't find that unusual? Even though my client owned the firm, weren't you responsible for compliance audits and signing off on submissions to Canada Revenue?" Jason asked.

"Well, yes, it was a bit unorthodox, but as you said, Barry owned the firm and could do as he pleased," Willard answered.

"But, didn't you, as Manager, have password access to all of the files on the server and the various computers in the office?" Jason asked.

"Yes, but the Andrews' account was encrypted and only Barry had the key," Willard responded.

"And you weren't the least bit curious or concerned?" Jason asked, getting ready to start pushing Willard hard about what he did and didn't know and do.

Willard shifted in his seat and said, "I've already testified that I spoke to Barry on several occasions about the locked Andrews' account and my concern that it should have some type of third party verification done by someone else in the office, just to check for any accidental errors before it's submitted to the CRA. Barry told me that was not necessary and basically told me to mind my own business and look after the rest of the accounts."

"You testified you suspected something was going on between my client and Ms. Ahmed, but never confirmed it and felt it wasn't any of your business anyway. Is that correct?" Jason asked.

"Yes, that's what I said," Willard responded.

"Can you tell the court a bit more about why you thought there was something more between my client and Ms. Ahmed than just a professional relationship?" Jason requested.

"I thought there were several more qualified candidates than Ms. Ahmed for the position we had open, but immediately after he met with her Barry insisted that she be hired," Willard said. "He took more than the usual interest in her orientation and I noted they spent a lot of time together in his office."

"Since they're the firm's biggest clients, I assume you know Jackson Andrews and his daughter Rose, my client's wife, fairly well?" Jason asked.

"Yes, I met them on a number of occasions," Willard answered.

"Did you ever discuss with them your concern about their account being locked up by my client and your suspicion he was having an affair with a young woman in the office?" Jason asked.

"Why would I do that?" Willard replied in a very defensive voice. "It was, as Barry told me, none of my business."

"You're a smart man, Mr. Willard, maybe also ambitious," Jason responded. "I spoke to other employees about you and they all agreed that you were the type of Manager who knew everybody's business and monitored their work very closely. You would have known the Andrews' account was very lucrative and big enough that a person could even start their own firm with it."

"What if I suggested to you that you did, in fact, whisper in Jackson Andrews' ear that his account was being compromised because my client was sleeping with and likely sharing secrets with Farah Ahmed. You thought that if you got in tight with the Andrews, they would push my client out and give you their account."

Before Willard attempted to respond, Shannon Renwick was on her feet and said, "Your Honour, despite your earlier warning, my colleague is at it again, making uncorroborated accusations for the jury to hear by building them into questions."

"Ms. Renwick is correct," Judge Paget, anger evident on his face, said to Jason. "I am again instructing members of the jury to disregard your comments during the questioning of this witness because they have no basis in fact. Mr. Burke, I will initiate contempt of court proceedings against you if I get even a hint you're trying this stunt again.

"Yes, Your Honour," Jason said. He didn't apologize because he did manage to plant a theory in the minds of the jurors. But he also realized he had pushed his defence strategy too far and would be severely restricted by the Judge going forward.

"I think you're done with this witness, Mr. Burke," Judge Paget said with contempt in his voice.

Chapter Sixteen - Present

Shane decided to get an early start working his way back through the Sterne file looking for things he might have missed, so he arrived at his King Street office shortly after 8 am the next day.

Shane thought he would have Burke and Associates to himself, but as he was walking to his office, he noticed the door was open and the light was on in Chioma Abiola's room. When he walked to her office and looked in, Chioma was at her desk on the left side of the room, her back turned to him, concentrating on her computer screen, so he knocked lightly on the door in order to not startle her.

Chioma turned, saw Shane, smiled, and said, "Good Morning, come on in."

"Good morning," Shane said and then held up the large take-out coffee he had in his right hand. "Sorry, if I knew you were here already, I would have brought you one of these," he said.

"I appreciate the thought, but I've already had way more coffee than normal this morning," Chioma responded.

"You've been working late and coming in early," Shane said. "You look tired, Chioma, you need to take some time off and recharge the battery."

"I will, but I've managed to put some information together for you and I thought we could go over it together this morning," She said. "Perhaps we can do it in your office where you have your list on the whiteboard."

Chioma grabbed her tablet and gathered her notes into a manila folder and she and Shane walked to his office where he rolled his chair out from behind his desk so they could sit beside each other.

Chioma then explained that she had completed updating the backgrounds of all of the major players in the Farah Ahmed murder case and would leave the file for Shane to review. She said some things had changed in the seven years since the Sterne trial, including his daughter Hanna getting married and having a child, Farah's ex-husband, Amir, re-married, and Bruce Willard, Sterne's Office Manager, had taken over the accounting business. The elderly neighbour, Edith McIntosh, who testified at the trial that she saw Sterne's car on the morning of the murder, passed away two years ago.

"Interestingly, Bruce Willard lists his home address as the same as Barry Sterne's former home where his wife, Rose, still lives," Chioma said.

"I know," Shane said, "I met with Rose at her house and Willard was there. I guess they've been an item for several years".

"Any chance they were involved at the time of Farah's murder?" Chioma asked. "That would add an interesting dynamic to the case if both Barry and Rose were involved with someone else."

"They both say no and got rather testy when I asked," Shane replied.

"I managed to get some updated information on Jackson Andrews and his company, but don't ask where some of it came from because you don't want to know," Chioma said with a smile.

Chioma was an outstanding researcher and one of the reasons why was because she had advanced computer skills that she used to hack into databases or find back doors into the systems used by companies and institutions. She told Shane that Andrews' warehouse and distribution firm continued to do very well and had even escaped the height of the pandemic relatively unscathed financially. She said Andrews has amassed a substantial personal fortune and in addition to owning several properties in Brantford, including the house where his granddaughter lived, he also had homes in Florida and in the Cayman Islands.

"The Cayman Islands property is convenient because he has a reason to travel there several times a year," Chioma said. "I'm not an expert, but when I looked over his bank records, and again you don't want to know how I did that, there appears to be money moving to offshore accounts to avoid taxes here."

"Not surprised," Shane said. "Avoiding taxes was one of the reasons Barry was manipulating the sales and inventory accounts, which Andrews denied knowing anything about."

"Andrews' wife, Emily, is an extremely private person and rarely seen in public," Chioma said. "I mention her because Andrews has his properties and most of his bank accounts in her name."

"Smart. A good way for him to shield himself if things go south, especially if he had been unsuccessful in shielding himself from the accounting fraud," Shane said.

"Now, let me fill you in on what I found out about the alibis," Chioma said.

Chioma told Shane that Farah's ex-husband, Amir, was on a construction site with about twenty other workers at the time of her murder. His new wife told police Amir was at home, in bed, when Barry Sterne and Jason were shot, so there's only her word for it.

Farah's father, Hassan Gupta, who made no secret of the fact he was very angry his daughter got divorced and had abandoned the Muslim faith, was out of the country when Farah was killed and at the local mosque with other worshippers when Sterne was shot.

"It's possible that someone else in either Amir's or her own family killed Farah because they believed she dishonoured them," Chioma said. "It would explain why there was no sign of forced entry because it was originally Amir's house, which Farah got in the divorce settlement, and Amir may still have had a key if Farah didn't change the locks."

"It's an excellent theory and I need to explore it further," Shane said. "It would explain Farah's murder, but I don't think anyone in the two families would be inclined to take revenge on Barry and Jason eight years later. That would mean they're two separate incidents."

Shane thought things over for a moment and then got up from his chair and added 'Amir and Farah families' to the list of names on the whiteboard hanging on the wall in his office.

Chioma then continued her report by saying both Jackson Andrews and his daughter Rose were at his business at the time of Farah's murder and when Sterne and Jason were shot. The daughter Hanna, who was seventeen at the time, was at Brantford Collegiate for an early morning class when Farah was killed and volunteering at her son's daycare when the recent shootings occurred.

"Police checked the security camera footage from all of the entrances and exits at Andrews' warehouse and office areas while investigating Farah's murder and it was included in the discovery that Jason received before Sterne's trial," Chioma said. "I went into the trial file and reviewed it again and it shows Andrews and Rose entering the office area separately prior to the time Farah was murdered and then not leaving until lunchtime. I double-checked footage of all of the other exits and they do not appear. Andrews and his daughter were apparently also at the office when Sterne was killed and Jason shot, so I'm assuming police have again checked the security footage, but we don't have access to that."

Chioma then smiled at Shane and added, "At least not legally."

Shane smiled back and said, "What have you done, Chioma, as if I couldn't guess."

"Andrews' security for his facility is handled by a private contractor called Shieldlink," Chioma answered. "But for a security company, they're not very secure."

Shane, who was more than competent with a computer, didn't understand half of what Chioma was saying as she explained how she was able to open a back door into the server Shieldlink used to store the video from the security cameras at Andrews' business.

"I reviewed the footage for the day Sterne and Jason were shot and I saw Andrews and Rose enter the office separately early in the morning and then leave together shortly after three in the afternoon," Chioma said. "So they both have an alibi."

"Same scenario as when Farah was murdered, so they're both ruled out for the two killings," Shane said.

"That may be true, but here's something to think about," Chioma responded. "I didn't find it particularly difficult to get into Shieldlink, so it would be easy for any halfway decent hacker. When I was in there, I could have easily manipulated the coding for security videos, perhaps change the dates and times, or even better, put a video loop on one of the exit cameras showing no activity to cover up someone leaving and entering the building."

"Can you tell if that's the case for the copy of the videos we have on file from eight years ago or can you go back into Shieldlink and look at the videos from last week?" Shane asked and then added, "I'm sure they would still have them on file."

"I can't, I don't have the expertise, especially if whoever did it was really good at it," Chioma replied and then said, "But I'm sure I can find someone if you want."

"I think so, but only do the videos we have on file because they were legally obtained during discovery for Sterne's trial," Shane said. "And even if there's a further chain of custody or admissibility issue, if the videos were tampered with it will narrow our focus to a couple of suspects, namely Jackson Andrews and his daughter Rose."

Chioma then said, "I've left what I think is the most interesting information until the end; the update on Eva Mendez, Farah's co-worker who claimed they were close friends and testified at the trial that Farah told her she feared for her life because of what she knew."

Chioma said Mendez quit working at Andrews' company shortly after the end of the Sterne trial, served her husband with divorce papers, packed up her belongings at their Fairview Street apartment, and moved out of Brantford with her twenty two year old son, Toby, who had been living with her.

"Do you know where she went?" Shane asked.

"I do," Chioma replied, "Are you ready for it? She moved to Port Elgin."

"You're kidding!" Shane exclaimed. Port Elgin was less than half an hour's drive from Shane's hometown of Paisley and it was where he went to high school.

"What are the chances of that?" Shane said to Chioma.

"She stays off social media, but I tracked her down through her son's Facebook account," Chioma said. "I did a property records search and she owns a large lakefront home on about an acre of property."

"That's very interesting. I wonder how she's able to afford that?" Shane questioned.

"Court filings show that when her divorce was finalized, there were very few assets to be divided," Chioma continued. "Her husband only worked sporadically but was ordered to pay alimony. And here's something else that's interesting; he's never made a payment, but Eva has made no attempt to go after him through the courts to get the money."

"Because she doesn't need the money. She has another source of income, a good one if she can afford a nice house," Shane said. "I wonder if she works?"

"I don't know, that's something that's difficult to track down online," Chioma responded.

Shane told Chioma that Mendez either left Brantford with a lot of money in the bank or is getting a steady influx of cash from somewhere, a clear indication that she was paid to lie at the Sterne trial about her friendship with Farah.

"I guess I'm off to Port Elgin to take a close look at Ms. Mendez," Shane said.

"Doesn't your foul-mouthed friend own a restaurant in Port Elgin, maybe he can help out?" Chioma said with a smile.

Shane smiled back and said, "Ben Chen? Maybe, because he knows the area and a lot of people. But he's never been a very politically correct guy, so I'll likely have to keep him from actually talking to anyone."

Chapter Seventeen- Present

The next day, Shane drove from Brantford to Paisley, making the trip in less than two and a half hours using some back roads he knew.

The air conditioning in the Charger hadn't worked for decades and even though it was early morning, it was a hot day already and it made for a noisy trip with the windows down in the classic muscle car.

On two occasions over the years, Shane had found a used compressor for the air conditioning at a scrapyard, but they never lasted very long so he gave up. Emma, who didn't like riding in the Charger at the best of times, refused to go anywhere in it during hot weather, preferring the comfort of her Jeep Grand Cherokee.

Paisley was a picturesque village, located at the junction of the Saugeen and Teeswater rivers, and noted for its historic town hall and small fire hall, which had been covered in bright red siding to protect it. The bridge in the middle of the village was being replaced and while it was well on its way to completion, the detour was still in place.

Shane had a love/hate relationship with his hometown.

Growing up, he and his best friend Ben loved walking their bikes up the inclined main street, stopping at various places along the way to buy candy or ice cream, and maybe going into the pool hall for a game of spots and stripes.

Once they reached the spot where the street started to level off heading out of Paisley, they would turn around, jump on their bikes, and start pedaling as hard as they could until they picked up enough downhill speed to cruise back through the village, legs out at the side of their bikes, their hair swept back by the wind, trying to avoid losing their balance and falling or, even worse, hitting a car. Shane and Ben also spent countless hours swimming, canoeing, and fishing along the Saugeen River.

But Paisley also held some dark memories for Shane.

At age seventeen, an uncle he didn't know that he had tried to kill him because Shane was investigating the disappearance of the man's young wife. Shane found her body in a shallow grave in a woodlot outside of town and many years later, dug up the body of his mother in the same area. He found out his uncle had murdered his mother and his father had killed his uncle's wife.

Thinking about these events was painful for Shane. Emma loved stopping in Paisley on their way to a vacation cottage in Port Elgin and visiting the gift and artisan shops, and Shane indulged this without complaint, but he always had a pit in his stomach.

Today, on the way northbound out of Paisley, Shane decided to stop at the service station at the edge of the village and fill up the Charger, a notorious gas guzzler. He pulled up to the pumps, got out of the car, and was met by the attendant, a thin older man with short gray hair and dark-rimmed glasses. Shane remembered him from the last time he had stopped there for gas. His name was Doug Connelly and he had told Shane that he retired from the Bruce Nuclear Station but didn't want to just sit at home.

"Hello, Mr. Connelly, you can fill it up," Shane said as the elderly man started pumping gas into the Charger.

"Shane Daniels! How are ya? And it's Doug, not Mr. Connelly, that's for old people," Connelly said with a big smile, his bushy eyebrows arching above the top frame of his glasses.

"I'm good Doug, thanks. You're still hanging around here, I see," Shane said.

Connelly chuckled and said, "My wife's not happy I'm working at my age, but I still can't bring myself to sit at home reading, doing jigsaw puzzles, and watching sports on television. And there's only so much yard work to do, so here I am."

"Hey, if it makes you happy working part-time pumping gas, I say good for you," Shane said.

"You're a bit of a celebrity around here," Connelly said as he completed filling Shane's car with fuel. "You know, because you solved the murders of those two ladies and got Ben Chen out of jail."

Connelly was referring to the murder of Ben's elderly next door neighbour in Paisley, Agnes McKinnon, as well as the killing of Janice Henderson on her farm near Kincardine. Ben was arrested for the McKinnon murder, but Shane connected her and Henderson's deaths to Alec MacDonald, a troubled young man living in horrid conditions on his deceased parent's farm in a rural area near Paisley.

"I was just trying to help my childhood friend," Shane said, deflecting the comment about being a celebrity. He handed Connelly his credit card to pay for the gas.

When Connelly returned with Shane's receipt he asked, "You here to solve another crime? I haven't heard about anything big in the area."

"No, just heading up to Port Elgin to visit some friends," Shane replied.

As he drove away from the gas station, Shane smiled and thought to himself that he should have told Mr. Connelly not to say anything to anybody, but he was working on a big case. Maybe he could have leaned in close to the senior and whispered, "Another murder, but keep it to yourself."

Shane grew up here, so he knew how things worked in a small town; some people had to know everyone else's business and he remembered that Doug Connelly used to be one of those people. So Shane figured he would have made the elderly man's day by telling him he was investigating a murder.

For sure, later in the day, Mr. Connelly would be sitting in the Legion drinking beer and telling his buddies he talked to Shane Daniels who filled him in on his latest case but swore him to secrecy. Then, after a couple of beers, Mr. Connelly wouldn't be able to help himself and would say, "Okay, but don't tell anyone…".

Less than half an hour later, Shane drove into Port Elgin, the popular tourist town on the shores of Lake Huron with a permanent population of about eight thousand but it swelled significantly during the summer months as vacationers jammed the area beaches.

Shane had called Ben to let him know he was coming and thought his friend would have been at his house in Paisley, perhaps working on coding for a video game, a hobby that had made Ben a lot of money over the years. Ben lived in his deceased parent's home on a street not far from the Saugeen River and Shane had thought he might have sold the house, considering it was beside the former home of the elderly woman Ben was accused of murdering. But Ben stayed and told Shane that if it caused tongues to keep wagging, then "fuck 'em".

When Shane called, Ben said he could stay at his house, but Shane had already managed to book a motel room in Port Elgin, lucky to find one during tourist season, but it helped that it was a weekday. Shane checked in and dropped off his overnight bag and then drove to Ben's restaurant, a popular Chinese buffet located on the southern edge of the town's downtown in an area of motels, restaurants, service stations, and convenience stores.

It was after 11 am and the parking lot at the buffet was already half full of customers for the reduced-priced luncheon. Shane parked the Charger and went inside, smiled at the Hostess at the reservation desk, who didn't stop him because she recognized Shane and knew he was there to see her boss.

Shane was surprised that Ben was at the restaurant because he had been staying away since he was cleared of the murder charge. Ben knew just the allegation he was involved in a crime would hurt his business and he figured being on site would just make matters worse.

Shane also knew that despite Ben's swear-filled bluster to the contrary, his friend had suffered emotionally during the time he had spent in jail and had lost a lot of his enthusiasm for being around people, sitting at his usual table just inside the dining area, and giving everyone a hard time.

When Shane walked in, Ben was at his usual spot and when he saw Shane he jumped up from his chair, a big smile on his face, and opened his arms for an embrace.

"Fucking-A, it's good to see you!" Ben said enthusiastically and loud enough that customers at several of the nearby tables looked up from their food to see what was going on.

The two men sat at Ben's table and he said, "How's Emma?"

"She's great," Shane answered and then added, "You know how much she loves it up here so she wanted to take time off work and come with me, but I told her it was strictly a quick working trip."

"Too bad, it would have been good to see her," Ben replied and Shane knew he was just saying that to be nice because it wasn't necessarily true. It wasn't that Ben and Emma disliked each other, far from it, but Ben sometimes felt that Emma was just putting up with him because he was Shane's oldest friend. Emma insisted she liked Ben, but Shane knew she was irked by his vocal social incorrectness and his inability to complete most sentences without a 'fuck' in it.

"I'd tell you to grab something to eat from the buffet, but that fucking slop is reheated leftovers from yesterday, so I wouldn't recommend it," Ben said, loud enough for some of the nearby customers to hear.

It wasn't true, of course, but was an example of Ben's weird sense of humour and one of the reasons, in addition to his foul language, why the second-generation Chinese Canadian was misunderstood by a lot of people, including Emma.

Ben immediately asked about Jason, saying how worried he was when he heard the lawyer had been shot. Jason represented Ben when he had been charged with murder and he both liked and respected the lawyer.

Shane said Jason was still in hospital but appeared to be recovering nicely and then went on to give Ben some basic background on the Farah Ahmed murder eight years ago and the recent shooting death of Barry Sterne. He said that he was in Port Elgin to look closely at a local resident, Eva Mendez, and explained how she fit into the case.

"I don't know the name, but there's a motherfucker sitting in the restaurant right now who might be able to help us out," Ben said. "He's the Sales Manager at the local GM dealership and sits on Saugeen Shores council, and the fucker probably knows just about everyone in town. Hang on and I'll go talk to him."

Ben got up from his chair and walked deep into the large dining area to a table with four men in suits sitting at it. Ben shook hands with one of them, a dark complected, middle-aged man with short cropped gray hair in a summer weight, light blue suit. Ben leaned over and spoke close to the man's right ear and the salesman started nodding in response and glanced over at Shane. After Ben was finished speaking, the man turned to face Ben and spoke. When he was done, Ben shook his hand again and returned to sit with Shane.

"That Sales Manager's name in Jim Watson, a bit of a self-centered prick, if you ask me," Ben said. "Anyway, he remembers that two years ago he sold a brand new Cadillac Escalade SUV to a town employee by the name of Josh Jacobs, who everybody apparently calls 'JJ'. It stood out to Watson because this fucking JJ paid cash and said he won money in the lottery."

"It must have been a big win because that Cadillac would have been at least a hundred thousand dollars," Shane said.

"Anyway, Watson told me that when they were filling out the address on the paperwork for the sale, JJ bragged that he was now living with a nice looking, well off, Spanish woman and her son at a house on the lake," Ben said. "The asshole couldn't remember the exact address this JJ filled out, but he thought it was Lakeview Avenue."

"That's the street where Eva Mendez bought her house," Shane said. "I'm thinking the lottery win is bullshit and Mendez put up the money for the Cadillac, but the vehicle would be in this JJ's name."

"So this Mendez woman is still getting paid for lying at the trial to help fuck Barry Sterne for the murder," Ben stated.

"That's what I think and it's what Jason believed at the time," Shane responded. "I need to confront Mendez and see if I can shake her up, but first I need to watch her for a bit."

Shane glanced over at the table where the four men were sitting and he noticed they were all looking his way. That prompted him to ask Ben, "How did you get that guy at the table over there to volunteer that information?"

"I lied," Ben answered, shrugging his shoulders. "I told him you were a friend of mine, a big city cop who was in town working on a case, and I was helping you out."

"You shouldn't have done that Ben," Shane admonished.

"Fuck'em," Ben responded.

Shane shook his head, smiled at his crazy friend, and then asked, "You up for doing a bit of surveillance?"

"Do ducks fucking swim? I'm totally your spy buddy," Ben replied enthusiastically.

Ben drove a huge Ford F150 pickup, which Shane thought his short, pudgy friend looked ridiculous in and was not very practical, but Ben had told him once why he did it and it was something only Ben would find amusing.

"You have to see the look on all the fucking rednecks around here when they see a chink driving by in what they consider to be their exclusive vehicle. It's fucking hilarious," Ben had told Shane.

Ben was a third-generation Chinese Canadian, but for some reason only known to him, he acted like he just arrived in the country, even though he didn't speak a word of either Cantonese or Mandarin. Shane had no idea how they had remained lifelong friends, they were extreme opposites, but right from the time they were little kids, Shane saw in Ben a trusted, loyal friend who never provided a dull moment.

They took Ben's truck because it was far less conspicuous for driving around Port Elgin than Shane's Charger, which never failed to get stared at wherever he went.

Eva Mendez's house on the aptly named Lakeview Street was a two-storey, brick home, with double front doors under a columned portico, and a two car garage at the end of a paved driveway. It had a wide, manicured front lawn and a colourful flower bed under the front bay window. The black Cadillac SUV was parked in the driveway and behind it a white pickup truck with Town of Port Elgin logos on the doors.

Ben parked his truck on the opposite side of the street and down half a block from the Mendez house and he and Shane spend a few minutes just looking. Between each house on the street, you could get a glimpse of the lake, its blue waters shimmering in the sunshine. It was a beautiful area.

Shane broke the silence when he said, "So a woman who rented an apartment in Brantford and worked as a clerk at an accounting firm, quits her job, divorces her husband, who didn't have any money by the way, and moves to Port Elgin to live in a house worth well north of a million dollars. What's wrong with that picture?"

"It's not fucking suspicious at all," Ben responded sarcastically and then asked, "And she owns that place?"

"Chioma checked the property records and her name is on the deed," Shane said and then added, "But she was going to do some digging into prior ownership, so let's call her and see if she found anything."

Shane took his cell phone out of his pocket and called the direct line into Chioma's office and she answered after one ring.

"Hi Shane, where are you," Chioma answered, Shane's name obviously coming up on her call display.

"Ben and I are sitting in his truck looking at Eva Mendez's beautiful, very expensive, lakefront home in Port Elgin," Shane answered.

"Has Ben said or done anything inappropriate yet?" she asked.

Shane glanced over at Ben as he answered, "He did make an out loud comment about the quality of the food in his restaurant, that's about it, but the day's only half over."

Ben, upon hearing this, smiled, shrugged his shoulders, and gave Shane the finger.

"If you're calling about the house, I think I've found something important," Chioma said. "The property was originally owned by a shell corporation registered in the Cayman Islands and it was a subsidiary of yet another shell corporation, so any attempt to find the actual owner leads nowhere. But, fifteen years ago, the property was purchased by a numbered company, which built the house."

"So, another dead end," Shane remarked.

"No, to be incorporated, a numbered company must have at least one Director and in this case, it's listed as Emily Hanson," Chioma said. "That's Jackson Andrews' wife's maiden name."

"Bingo! Great work, Chioma," Shane reacted. "The house was one of the many properties Andrews bought to hide his money and he gives it and cash to Eva Mendez to testify at the Sterne trial," he said.

"The records show the house was sold for one point one million dollars and I'm sure all of the paperwork would show that, but no money would have actually exchanged hands," Chioma said.

"Thanks, Chioma, this is exactly the kind of leverage I need. You're the best!" Shane exclaimed.

"You keep saying that, maybe someday I'll actually believe you," Chioma responded in her typical humble way.

As soon as Shane hung up, Ben asked him, "Did she say something fucking bad about me?"

"Just the usual that everyone says, Ben," Shane told him.

"Oh, well, that's okay then," Ben said.

Shane then filled his friend in on what Chioma found out about the house and property, and they both agreed the connection between Andrews and Mendez should kick start the process of finding out who really killed Farah Ahmed and likely murdered Barry Sterne and shot Jason Burke.

While they were talking, they watched as a man walked out the front door of the house, got in the Town truck, and drove away. It was just before 1 pm, so they figured Mendez's partner must have been home for lunch. Josh 'JJ' Jacobs was a big man, a least six feet tall, with the build of someone who was no stranger to manual labour. He had a dark tan from working outside, short sandy brown hair, a boxer's nose, and deep set eyes. He was wearing tan work boots, dark green work pants, and a short sleeve green button-up shirt under a bright orange reflector safety vest.

With the Cadillac still in the driveway, Shane figured there was a chance that Mendez was home and he felt it would be a good time to make initial contact with the woman, tell her what he knew about the house she was living in, which was well above her means, and gauge her reaction.

Ben wanted to tag along for the meeting but Shane said it wasn't a good idea, two men showing up at the door unannounced. It would be too intimidating.

"Yea, like anyone would be afraid of a fucking short, fat, Chinese guy," Ben said facetiously.

"Just stay here, please Ben," Shane said, always amused by Ben's self-deprecating humour.

Shane got out of the truck, crossed the street, walked along the sidewalk, then down the driveway to the double front door where he rang the doorbell. A small dog inside started barking, he heard someone telling it to shut up, and then the deadbolt turned on the door.

Shane had never met Eva Mendez in person, but he had seen her photo in Jason's file from the Sterne trial. The woman who opened the door had not changed much over the past seven years with the exception of her hairstyle, no longer pulled back and tied in a bun like in the picture, but now down on her shoulders, parted in the middle of her head, and no gray showing. She no longer wore glasses, so Shane assumed she now had contacts.

"Can I help you?" Mendez asked.

"Ms. Mendez, my name is Shane Daniels and I work with Jason Burke, the lawyer who represented Barry Sterne at the Ahmed murder trial seven years ago."

"I know who Jason Burke is," Mendez said flatly.

"Well, I don't know if you've heard or not, but several days ago Barry Sterne was shot and killed shortly after he was released from prison, and Mr. Burke was shot and wounded in a separate incident."

"What's that got to do with me," Mendez said and Shane saw her eyes narrow and he knew he had arrived at the make it or break it moment that would determine if their conversation would go any further.

"I believe the two shootings are connected to Farah Ahmed's murder and the Sterne trial back in 2016 and I wanted to talk to you about those events, to get your perspective because you worked at Sterne's firm with Farah and you testified at the trial about your relationship," Shane said, trying to be calm and friendly.

"I'm sorry to hear about Sterne and your boss, but as I said, its got nothing to do with me. I have nothing to say to you," Mendez said and started closing the door.

Shane quickly put his hand on the door to stop it from closing, and then said, "Ms. Mendez, Eva, I know that you realize the time has come for you to put things right because not only have I found you, but I've found you living in a million dollar home we both know you could never afford on a clerk's salary and you're driving a high-end luxury vehicle that was paid for with cash. And don't try telling me you won the lottery because the OLG always releases the names of big winners for publicity and your name is not on the list."

"I inherited some money," Mendez said defiantly.

"No you didn't," Shane responded in a firm voice. "I checked. Your grandparents and parents passed away a long time ago and if they left you a lot of money, you would have been living like this well before the Sterne trial."

Nothing was said for several moments as Shane continued to hold the door open with his hand and Mendez stared at him. Then Shane saw the defiant look on her face disappear and her eyes moisten with tears, and he thought that his gamble on confronting her might have worked.

"I'm so sorry that Barry got murdered, I didn't mean for that to happen," Mendez said as tears started running down her cheeks.

"Eva, I know who owned this house when you got it, it's going to come out and it's going to prove you were paid to lie on the stand at the trial about your relationship with Farah and what she told you," Shane said. "You need to get ahead of this right now and not end up being the only one who takes the blame for what happened to Barry Sterne."

Shane was bluffing. He had no idea if Jackson Andrews' wife's name on the numbered company that once owned the house was enough to convince the police to open an investigation into Mendez's testimony at a trial seven years ago. But he hoped Mendez wouldn't see it that way.

It turned out he was right, because Mendez stepped back, opened the door the entire way, and said, "You better come in."

Shane and Mendez sat in the home's spacious living room and talked for over half an hour. Mendez said in the time period shortly before

Farah's murder, she had become increasingly desperate for money, her deadbeat husband wasn't working a lot, they were two months behind on the rent for their apartment and the landlord was making noise about starting the eviction process. Bruce Willard, the Office Manager at Sterne's firm knew she was having financial problems because she had been forced to ask for an advance on her salary on several occasions.

After Barry was arrested and charged with Farah's murder, Mendez said she got a call out of the blue from Jackson Andrews, a man she had seen in the office on many occasions but had never been introduced to. Andrews told her that Willard had mentioned to him that she was struggling financially and he wanted to help her out. He said that Willard would offer her a solution and she should know that it came from him.

"Andrews went through Willard so he would have deniability if it ever came out about what he wanted you to do," Shane said.

"I guess so," Mendez replied.

Mendez then explained that Willard called her into his office the next day and offered her two hundred thousand dollars if she would tell the police, and then testify at the trial, that she and Farah were good friends, Farah had told her about her affair with Barry, and that she feared for her life because of what she knew was going on at the firm.

"Two hundred thousand dollars is a lot of money," Shane said. "If you were desperate financially that should have been enough to get you to do what they wanted, but you also ended up with this house. How did that happen?"

"Because when Willard offered me the money, I said no," Mendez answered. "I needed the cash badly, but I wasn't sure if I could go through with the lie. I always liked Barry and even though I believed, like everybody else, that he killed Farah, I didn't know if I wanted to be part of putting him in jail for it."

"So Willard, on Andrews' behalf, offered you this house and the cash, and then you were more than happy to lie," Shane said.

He realized he had used a very judgmental tone of voice and immediately regretted it. He needed to keep Mendez talking and criticizing the choice she made could jeopardize that.

"I admit that when I was offered a free house in a town where I could start all over and nobody would know me, I did what I did without a second thought," Mendez said. "You don't have to believe me, but after I moved in here not a month went by when I didn't have a spell of deep depression over what I did. I finally had to lie to a doctor to get some pills to help me over the rough patches. There have been a couple of times over the years that if it wasn't for what it would do to my son, I was prepared to go back to Brantford and admit what I had done."

"I'm curious," Shane said. "Did you ever think about why Jackson Andrews was so determined to get you to lie that he would give you a lot of money and a million dollar lakefront home?"

"Oh, I was pretty sure I knew why right from the start," Mendez answered. "I think Andrews thought that maybe it was his daughter Rose who actually murdered Farah. He would do anything to protect Rose, and that meant making sure Barry was found guilty."

Shane sat forward on the couch he was on so he was closer to Mendez in her chair, then said, "Eva, I need you to understand something. At the time of the trial, Jason Burke was convinced that Barry didn't kill Farah, but he couldn't prove it, and all of the circumstantial evidence and testimony, particularly yours, was stacked against his client."

Shane let Mendez think about that for a moment and then said, "You have an important decision to make and I don't want to force you to make it by providing the police with the information I have on this house and your income. It would be in your favour to come forward voluntarily and make a statement."

Mendez's tears had dried up and the look on her face told Shane she was quickly considering her options and he started to worry that she might call his bluff over what information against her that he could or couldn't provide the authorities.

"I have to think about it," Mendez finally said.

"You do that, but keep in mind what I just said I would do if you don't come forward," Shane said, deciding to double down on his bluff.

Shane stood up to go and then said, "Eva, Barry Sterne spent seven years in prison for a murder I don't believe he committed and then he gets killed, likely by someone who wanted revenge or to make sure he never attempted to clear his name. Well, Barry deserves to have his name cleared and you can help do that."

Mendez didn't say anything as she walked Shane to the door and just before he walked out, Shane took his business card out of his pocket, handed it to her, and said, "My number is on there. I'm staying in town until noon tomorrow so call me if you've decide what you're going to do or if you want to talk about it again. But don't take too long to make up your mind."

When he returned to the truck, Ben was staring intently at his phone, his thumbs working at a rapid pace on the keyboard. When Shane climbed into the tall vehicle, Ben set his phone on its dashboard holder and asked, "How'd it go?"

"I think she's going to make a statement to police that she was paid to lie at the trial," Shane answered.

"How the fuck did you get her to do that!" Ben asked in surprise.

"I convinced her that if she didn't come forward voluntarily, I would provide the police with proof of her guilt," Shane answered.

"You could do that?" Ben asked.

"Not really," Shane responded. "All I really have is Jackson Andrew's wife's name on a numbered company that used to own the property. I just sort of intimated I had more."

"You are one devious fuck. I love it," Ben said, his face all lit up in excitement. He then asked, "What now?"

"I told her she needed to make her mind up before I left town tomorrow. Fingers crossed it will work," Shane said. "Meantime, let's get something to eat. I would suggest Chinese, but I hear the buffet in town is really bad."

"I do the fucking Chinese food jokes," Ben said, faking a look of indignation on his face.

"Sorry," Shane replied with a smile.

Chapter Eighteen - Present

Shane didn't hear back from Eva Mendez the rest of that day and wondered if he was going to have to go back to her house and try and talk to her again. He knew the whole thing was a gamble that might not pay off.

He and Ben decided on steak for an early dinner, which Shane knew was his friend's preference after Ben started alluding to the mysterious ingredients in the food at his buffet. After their meal, they drove around Port Elgin for a while, including down Elgin Street to the public beach and to the marina to check out the various expensive pleasure craft docked there.

Late in the day, Ben dropped him off at his motel and Shane called Emma to let her know he would hopefully be home sometime the next afternoon and to fill her in on his meeting with Eva Mendez.

"If she hasn't called you back by now, do you assume she has no intention of admitting what she did and implicating Jackson Andrews and Bruce Willard?" Emma asked.

"She claimed that she had been haunted over the years by what she did to Sterne and early in our conversation she was genuinely emotional about it," Shane responded and then added, "But later, when I was about to leave, I could see her mental wheels turning as she was undoubtedly trying to think if there was a way to keep the status quo.

Or maybe she was trying to decide if I really could prove what I claimed."

Shane and Emma talked for another twenty minutes, mostly about what she had been up to, and the current gossip around the hospital. Emma said she had been in to see Jason a couple of times and he continued to recover with hope he could be discharged by the end of the week with some at-home wound care set up for him.

Shane was exhausted from the day's events, the drive from Brantford to Port Elgin, and the stress over trying to talk Eva Mendez into making a statement to the police. He went to bed early and slept a lot later than normal.

In the morning, there still wasn't a call from Mendez and Shane was trying to decide whether or not to go back to her house and try again. He checked out of the motel and was on his way to the Charger in the parking lot when he saw two men standing by the trunk of the car, obviously waiting for him.

He recognized one of the men right away as Josh 'JJ' Jacobs, Eva Mendez's boyfriend, and he assumed the other man was Toby Mendez, Eva's son because he looked like her; dark complected, with black hair and dark brown eyes.

"Good morning, can I help you gentlemen?" Shane asked pleasantly as he approached them and stopped.

"I'm glad to see that you're leaving town, I'm here to make sure you did that, and to tell you not to come back, to stay away from Eva Mendez, and never contact her again," Jacobs said.

Up close, Shane confirmed what he saw from Ben's truck yesterday; Jacobs was a powerfully built man, with muscular arms and a broad chest. But, he was also carrying a lot of extra weight based on a big gut hanging over his belt. Toby Mendez was also a big guy, just under six feet tall with broad shoulders and a wide waist.

Eva must have told JJ and her son about my visit with her yesterday, Shane thought, and they had come to try and physically intimidate him. He wondered if Eva knew they were here.

"You must be Josh Jacobs, Eva's partner, and I assume you're her son, Toby," Shane said, again trying to stay pleasant, although he figured this encounter was going to be far from that.

"It doesn't matter who we are as long as you understand what I just told you," Jacobs said in a threatening tone.

Toby didn't say anything but did take a step forward from his position slightly behind Jacobs so that the two men were now side-by-side and within arms reach of Shane.

"So, what, JJ, can I call you JJ?, you and Toby are going to beat me up if I don't do what I'm told?" Shane asked.

"Something like that," Jacobs replied and Shane noted that both men had balled their hands into fists and taken another step closer to him, all part of the intimidation they were attempting.

"You'd have no problem beating up a handicapped man?" Shane asked as he tossed his walking cane from his left to right hand, grabbed it about halfway up the shaft, and held it straight out from his body for both men to see.

"Doesn't bother me if that cripple is an asshole who needs to stay out of other people's business," Jacobs replied.

"Just checking," Shane said.

Shane knew a lot about knees because he had one that had been damaged beyond restoration by a shotgun. The knee is the largest and most complex joint in the human body and is made up of four things: bones, cartilage, ligaments, and tendons. The only protection is the patella, the kneecap, and the area all around it is vulnerable to injury. For example, the ligaments and tendons that hold the knee in place aren't strong enough to withstand any quick, hard lateral movement. It would be even worse if you were a big guy carrying extra weight that put extra pressure on your knees. There was also the medial meniscus on the inside of the knee and the lateral meniscus on the outside, both acting as shock absorbers, which would lock up and swell if damaged.

Because he knew all that, and because he also knew he didn't stand a chance against the two big men facing him, Shane didn't hesitate.

In one very fast sequence, Shane tossed his cane, which he was holding by the shaft, straight up, grabbed the end of it in both hands, swung it like a baseball bat with everything he had, and smashed the handle into the soft spot just below and left of Jacobs kneecap. Jacobs yelled out in pain and his knee gave out. But to ensure Jacobs didn't attempt to respond, Shane quickly pulled his cane back and dealt a crushing blow to the man's other knee. This time, Jacobs went down hard to the ground, writhing in agony.

Shane figured Toby would be shocked by his sudden, violent attack on Jacobs and would likely hesitate before making a move. That's exactly what Toby did and during that hesitation, Shane pulled back his cane and thrust it straight ahead, ramming the handle into the young man's crotch. Like Jacobs, Toby cried out in pain, dropped to the ground, and cupped his damaged genitals in his hands.

Shane leaned over Jacobs, who was rolling back and forth in agony with one hand over each knee, and said, "Listen up JJ. You're going to be laid up for a while, but if you decide to send Toby over there, or anyone else, to threaten me again, I will do a lot worse than just bust a knee and bruise some balls."

Shane got in the Charger and because no one was parked in front of him, he was able to drive straight ahead, leaving the two men on the ground at the rear of his vehicle.

After leaving the motel parking lot, Shane drove along the main street until he found the first open parking spot and stopped. Now that the confrontation was over, the adrenalin rush Shane had felt had dissipated and both shock and exhaustion had taken its place. Sweat started running down his face and Shane gripped the steering wheel hard to keep his hands from shaking. He was no stranger to violence and had used his cane very effectively in the past to defend himself, but that didn't make it any easier to deal with the aftermath.

Shane grabbed a couple of napkins he had in the glove box and wiped the sweat from his face. Jacobs and Toby coming after him meant that Eva Mendez didn't believe he could prove she was bribed to testify at the Sterne trial. But Shane wasn't about to give up because getting Mendez to come forward would implicate Jackson Andrews and Bruce Willard in a conspiracy to frame Barry Sterne and open the door to finding out who actually murdered Farah Ahmed then killed Sterne and wounded Jason Burke eight years later.

Shane decided he would drive to Mendez's house right away and pressure her some more, this time telling her that sending her boyfriend and son to assault him would be further proof he would provide authorities to have her arrested for her part in the conspiracy against Sterne.

Now that he was able to calm himself down, Shane was about to pull away from the curb when his phone rang. The call display said, 'E. Mendez'.

"Hello, Eva, sending JJ and Toby to beat me up didn't work. They're both going to need medical attention," Shane said.

"What are you talking about? I called to tell you I was ready to make a statement," Mendez said and Shane could hear the confusion in her voice.

"JJ and your son just tried to assault me in the parking lot of my motel," Shane said and then asked, "You didn't know about that?"

"No, I didn't, the idiots," Eva answered. "Last night, I told them everything and said I felt responsible for the murder of a man I helped send to prison and that I was going to try and put things right by confessing what I did so that at least Barry's name would be cleared."

"They obviously didn't take it too well," Shane said.

"They were both angry," Eva said. "JJ said everything you told me was bullshit and that you couldn't prove anything. Toby said he had always been suspicious after we left his father and moved into the house here with lots of money to spend, but he didn't say anything because suddenly his life was a lot better. And while he said he was angry that I ruined another man's life and likely caused his death, he was even angrier that I was prepared to throw away everything we now enjoyed."

"So they decided to take matters into their own hands," Shane said.

"They're both not the brightest bulbs. I'm sorry," Mendez said.

"It doesn't matter, Eva. I'm on my way to your house right now to pick you up and we'll go to the Saugeen Shores Police and have an officer take your statement," Shane said.

After he disconnected the call, Shane tapped his fist against the steering wheel and said softly, but enthusiastically, "Yes!" This would break the case wide open and start the process of getting some questions answered.

Shane was about to put the Charger in gear when his phone rang again. The display said 'unknown caller'.

"Shane Daniels," he answered.

"Mr. Daniels, this is Father Hennepin calling from the Millhaven Hospice for prisoners. I'm sorry to inform you that your father has passed away."

Chapter Nineteen - 2016

Jason Burke couldn't believe that against his better judgement, he had finally agreed to let Barry Sterne take the stand in his own defence.

But it was too late to change his mind because Barry was already in the witness box ready for the Prosecutor's questions.

Barry had been pushing Jason to let him testify since the beginning of the trial, but Jason repeatedly told him it was a bad idea and would open him up to a lot of compromising questions that would make him look guilty to the jury. Barry thought that if he didn't testify the jury would assume he was guilty, but Jason countered by saying members of the jury would be well aware through crime movies and TV, albeit American, that defendants in criminal trials often don't testify.

At the end of the day yesterday when the prosecution had completed presenting its case, Jason and Barry spent over an hour in a small attorney-client meeting room at the courthouse debating the pros and cons of Barry taking the stand.

Jason told him that it was guaranteed the Prosecutor would link his accounting fraud and his affair with Farah as proof he couldn't be trusted to tell the truth on the stand.

"Barry, you come across as a sincere guy, which is good, and even if you answer the questions truthfully, if any of the jurors get even the smallest inkling that you may be lying, they'll vote to convict," Jason said. "It's a huge risk to take."

"But I've been painted as a man who viciously stabbed his girlfriend to death because he was afraid she was going to squeal on him about his illegal activities," Barry countered. "It's not true. I loved Farah deeply and wanted to spend the rest of my life with her. I would never hurt her. I need to say that to the jury."

"And you'll get a chance to do that during my cross-examination, but it may be too late if the Prosecutor, and Shannon Renwick is a good one, tears you to shreds first," Jason said.

"I'm willing to take my chances," Barry responded.

"But if I keep you off the stand, we don't have to take that chance," Jason said. "We let the fact that they have no murder weapon, no direct evidence linking you to the murder other than DNA at the crime scene, which would be expected to be there since you were lovers, and testimony from some witnesses that I believe I have shown to have ulterior motives."

"Jason, don't get me wrong, I think you have done an excellent job on my behalf," Barry said. "But I'm not blind, I see how the jurors are looking at me and their faces say 'guilty'. You know that's true. Taking the stand and letting them see and hear who I truly am may be the only shot I have."

Jason knew what Barry was saying was true, but he very rarely let a client take the stand in their own defence because he knew more often than not they couldn't withstand a Prosecutor's intense scrutiny. However, he was also aware that his strategy of attacking the credibility of prosecution witnesses had only been partially successful and may have even turned some of the jurors against him.

"Barry, I admit that things don't look good right now," Jason said. "So I think I'm obligated to again suggest that instead of you taking the stand, I see if the Crown would accept a guilty plea on the reduced charge of manslaughter in exchange for substantially less time in prison than the automatic twenty five years you would get for second-degree murder. They might be willing to agree to that in order to claim victory and not leave it in the hands of the jury."

"I will never plead guilty to something I didn't do," Barry said intensely. "I'm guilty of cheating on my wife and guilty of accounting fraud, which I will accept my punishment for, but I'm willing to spend the rest of my life in prison before I will agree to say I killed the woman I loved. I didn't do it."

"It's okay, Barry, I understand," Jason said softly in an effort to calm Barry down. "If it's what you want, I will prepare you the best I can and you can take the stand."

So, before court today, Jason spend an hour telling Barry what he could expect on the stand and had him answer some practise questions.

Then the court session began and Shannon Renwick got up from her chair, walked to an area halfway between her table and Barry in the witness box, and began her examination.

Normally, since he was a defence witness, Jason would question Barry before the Prosecutor, but he requested and was granted by Judge Paget to allow Renwick to go first.

Jason didn't want to question Barry and then watch him undergo the expected grilling by the Prosecutor, which would force him to do a follow-up in an attempt to repair any of Barry's damaging testimony. By then, any good Barry's original testimony had achieved would be lost on the jury. Better to get all of the bad stuff out of the way first and then work with Barry on the stand to leave a good final impression.

"Mr. Sterne," Renwick started, "The court has heard from several witnesses that you're considered a brilliant accountant, a genius when it comes to numbers, balance sheets, financial statements, and tax preparation. That's mighty high praise, wouldn't you agree?"

"I don't know about genius, but I've had an affinity with numbers as long as I can remember and found that accounting work came easy for me. I've been lucky that way," Barry answered.

"I guess you found committing fraud easy to do as well?" Renwick asked.

"Your Honour," Jason said as he stood up at his table. "The accounting fraud at my client's firm was part of the agreed statement of facts at the start of this trial. My client is not on trial for fraud and should not be subject to continuous questioning about it by my colleague."

Renwick turned to the Judge and said, "Your Honour, we have provided witness testimony that Farah Ahmed's threat to go to the authorities about the fraud was the motive for Mr. Sterne stabbing her to death. I assume Mr. Sterne has taken the stand in his own defence to try and refute that. Therefore, I should be allowed to question him about the fraud and its link to the victim."

"I agree," Judge Paget ruled and then said to Jason, "Mr. Burke, by taking the stand your client has opened the door to all questions surrounding the circumstances leading up to the murder." The Judge then said to Renwick, "But, Ms. Renwick, let's not belabour already agreed to facts."

"Yes, your Honour," Renwick said and then turned back to face Barry.

"Mr. Sterne, I just want you to clarify something for the court. Do you dispute the fact that you told Ms. Ahmed about the fraud going on with the Andrews' accounts and she threatened to go to the authorities?"

"I don't dispute that I told Farah about what was going on, but only after she shared her suspicions and started asking questions," Barry replied. "What I strongly dispute is that she intended to inform the police and that I somehow threatened her life if she did that. That simply didn't happen. I wanted to leave my wife and be with Farah, but she felt I needed to get clear of my illegal activities first and we were still discussing how to do that when she was killed."

"And these so-called discussions also included arguments loud enough for the neighbours to hear?" Renwick asked sarcastically.

"We did have some heated disagreements over the timing of my coming forward about the fraud, but they never lasted long. They happened because we really cared about each other and were passionate about our future," Barry answered.

Sitting at the defence table, Jason thought that Barry was doing really well so far. He was keeping his answers short and not offering anything more than what he was asked. He was keeping his emotions in check, with no anger or indignation, but Jason had told him it was okay to show some emotion when talking about his relationship with Farah.

"Mr. Sterne, you told police you drove to Ms. Ahmed's house during the time the coroner testified that she was murdered, but you didn't go in and see her," Renwick said. "But her neighbour testified there was a length of time between when you went by her house on your way to Ms. Ahmed's and when she saw you going back the other way, driving fast like you were trying to get away. How do you explain that gap in time? Did you, in fact, go into the house, stab Ms. Ahmed multiple times, and then tried to leave the area in a hurry?"

Jason knew he could have objected several times during Renwick's question, accusing her of using inflammatory language, but he chose not to. He didn't want to keep interrupting and give the jury the impression he was trying to keep Barry from answering the tough questions.

"I had planned to go into the house, but I changed my mind," Barry answered. "After a lot of soul searching, I had decided to confess the accounting manipulation I had been doing for years. I wanted to tell Farah my decision because I knew it would make her happy."

"But when I got to the house, I had second thoughts and stopped my car a couple of houses up from Farah's. I sat there for a while, I don't know how long, thinking about all of the ramifications of what I was planning to do, and the impact on my family. And I admit I was scared, knowing I would likely go to jail. I decided I needed more time to think, so I drove home."

"You had a key to Ms. Ahmed's house, correct?" Renwick asked.

"Yes, it was so I could let myself in if Farah wasn't home yet and I wouldn't have to wait for her in my car," Barry answered.

Jason knew she was doing it for dramatic purposes as he watched Renwick go to her table, pick up a manila folder, look at the papers inside, then said to Barry, "Mr. Sterne, do you recall when the forensics officer from the Brantford Police Service testified that there was no sign of forced entry into Ms. Ahmed's house?"

"I do remember that, yes," Barry replied.

"How do you explain that?" Renwick asked.

"I can't," Barry responded. "Maybe someone managed to get a copy of her key or maybe she answered the door and the killer forced their way in."

"But Ms. Ahmed was murdered in her bed and there was no sign of a struggle anywhere else in the house," Renwick responded.

"I don't know what happened, I just know that I didn't do it," Barry replied, his voice starting to rise in irritation, but to Jason's relief, he could see Barry trying to stay calm.

Renwick then said, "Isn't it more likely that you were sitting in your car outside Farah's house because you had changed your mind about confessing your fraud. You had decided you still wanted the extra money and you didn't want to go to jail."

"But," Renwick continued, "Farah could ruin everything because she's said she would go to the authorities if you didn't. So you used your key to let yourself into her house, a house you're very familiar with and knew exactly where the bedroom was, and you went in there where Farah was sleeping and stabbed her, many times."

"That's not true, I would never do that!" Barry exclaimed. "I loved Farah, I would never hurt her!"

"Mr. Sterne," Renwick continued, "You're an admitted financial fraudster who cheated on his wife. Why should we believe anything you say?"

Enough is enough, Jason thought and started to get to his feet to object, but Judge Paget put up his hand and said, "Don't bother, Mr. Burke, your client put himself in this position. Please answer the question, Mr. Sterne."

"It's fine, your Honour," Renwick interrupted before Barry could say anything. We already know the answer. I'm finished with this witness."

Jason stood up quickly and said with indignation in his voice, "Your Honour, you've admonished me several times during this trial for making statements instead of questions. Should the same not apply to my colleague?"

"I'll ignore your criticism of my rulings, Mr. Burke, and agree," Judge Paget said with irritation in his voice. He then turned to the jury and said, "The jury will disregard the Prosecutor's last statement. Mr. Burke, you may begin your questioning of the witness."

Jason was just trying to make a point because he knew it never made any sense when a Judge told a jury to ignore something that was said. How do you unhear something?

"I only have a few questions, your Honour," Jason said, and turning to the witness box, he asked, "Barry, did you kill Farah Ahmed?"

Jason had decided to use Sterne's first name in his questions to help humanize Barry and show there was a close bond and friendship between them. He wanted the jurors to wonder why a lawyer with his reputation would defend a man who viciously stabbed a woman to death if he wasn't innocent. It was a small ploy, but Jason needed to try anything he could to put reasonable doubt in the minds of the jurors.

"No, I did not," Barry answered in a firm voice as he looked directly at the jury. "I had fallen deeply in love with Farah and I know she felt the same way. I would never hurt her."

"But you had second thoughts about publicly admitting your accounting fraud, which Farah wanted you to do, and you drove away from her house without going in the morning she was killed," Jason stated.

"I realized that I needed more time to think things through, to have a better plan in place to handle the fallout," Barry said.

"I started the relationship with Farah because I no longer had one with my wife," he said. But, you have to understand that while my marriage to Rose was over, I didn't hate her, we had some great years together and produced a daughter, Hanna, who I love very much. I was about to hurt them deeply in a very public manner, so I needed to talk to them first before I did anything. They deserved at least that much. I wasn't confident I knew how to do that, and that's why I left Farah's house without seeing her."

"Just one final, but important, question Barry," Jason said. "Farah's co-worker, Eva Mendez, claimed she and Farah had become close friends and she testified that Farah told her she feared for her life because of what she knew about illegal activity at your firm. Were you aware they were so close that Farah would tell her that?"

"I have no idea why Eva claimed Farah said that, because it's not true," Barry replied. "Farah had nothing to fear regarding her suspicions because she knew I loved her. When she came to me with what she suspected, I wasn't upset, because I knew that day would eventually arrive. I was impressed that Farah was the one smart enough to figure it out. There were never any threats.

"The thing is," Barry continued, "I never saw Farah and Eva hanging around together in the office or even talking. And not once when we were together did Farah even mention Eva's name. I don't know Eva's motive for saying what she did, but I do know they're not true and that she and Farah were not friends."

"Thank you, Barry, that's all the questions I have," Jason responded, and then turning to the Judge, he said, "The defence rests, your Honour."

Chapter Twenty - Present

Shane figured it was almost always either overcast or raining at graveside services in the movies, but more often than not, that was not the case.

He thought about this as the sun beat down on him and made him sweat in his dark suit as he stood at his father's grave at Douglas Hill Cemetery on Bruce Road 3 south of Paisley.

It was late morning, already a hot day, and in addition to dealing with the sweat running down his face, Shane had to continually slap at the mosquitoes landing on his face from the cloud of them surrounding his head.

Emma on his right and Ben on his left were dealing with the same uncomfortable situation. Emma was wearing a nice summer weight, but dark, pantsuit, and Ben was in jeans with a sport coat, white shirt, and dark, thin tie.

They were the only ones at the grave site, looking down at the dark brown coffin with the silver handrails sitting on a mat of artificial turf over the open grave. Two cemetery workers stood a respectful distance away, waiting to lower the coffin into the ground when Shane, Emma, and Ben left.

The two days leading up to this point had been a bit crazy for Shane.

All kinds of things were running through his head when Father Hennepin called to tell him his father had died, but he was determined to do one thing first before he dealt with his father's death.

He travelled to Eva Mendez's house, picked her up, and drove to the Saugeen Shores Police Service headquarters. He explained the situation to the Staff Sargent at the front desk who said he wasn't sure if there was anyone available to do what Shane wanted. Shane knew he couldn't afford a delay in getting Eva to make her statement because he knew she was very nervous, he could see her hands shaking as she held her purse, and he was worried she was going to change her mind.

Shane got verbally aggressive with the Staff Sargent, telling him he didn't want to drive to the RCMP detachment in Owen Sound and let the Mounties get the credit for helping solve a major murder case, but he would. The Staff Sargent, realizing his superiors wouldn't be happy if they found out that happened, called a Constable to come and cover the front desk, and personally took Shane and Eva to an interrogation room where he took her statement, plus videotaped it.

After he had a copy of the typed statement and the videotape in his possession, Shane drove Eva home and spent half an hour discussing with her what he planned to do with them, and advising her to be prepared for the police to show up at her door.

Shane didn't see JJ or Toby, and Eva didn't mention them, which he was glad about, and he thought perhaps they were staying out of the way in another part of the house. JJ would most certainly still be in a lot of pain from the damage inflicted on his knees by Shane.

When he got back to his motel, Shane was able to re-book his room for several more days and then called Emma and told her about his father. She said she would drive up to Port Elgin right away to join him and Shane told her he would call the funeral home in Paisley to get arrangements underway to have his father's body transported there from Kingston.

Shane then called Sgt. Mark Stabler at the Brantford Police Service, explained what he had obtained, and said Eva's written statement and videotape were being delivered to him by the Saugeen Shores Police Service using an official chain of custody process.

"I thought I told you to stay out of the Sterne murder and Jason's shooting," Stabler said on the phone.

"First of all, I did stay out of it. I've been looking into the Farah Ahmed murder," Shane replied. "Second of all, a 'thank you' would be nice for handing you something that presents a lot of questions about who may have actually killed Farah and likely murdered Sterne."

"What? You want a thank you for throwing a monkey wrench into an eight year old murder case and potentially embarrassing Brantford Police if it turns out we got it wrong?" Stabler replied.

"This isn't about embarrassing anyone," Shane responded. "Jackson Andrews, through Bruce Willard, paid Eva Mendez to testify against

Barry Sterne, either because he was afraid his daughter had actually murdered Farah Ahmed, or he did it, or had someone do it for him. This is about finding out which one it was and possibly clearing an innocent man's name."

"Okay, Okay, Shane, I don't need a lecture on doing the right thing. You know me well enough to know that's exactly what I'll do," Stabler responded defensively. "Once I get the material, I'll review it and then I'll have to bring Andrews and Willard in for questioning, probably both with their lawyers."

"Now I need a favour," Shane stated.

"A favour! You're kidding, right? After you stirred up this shit?" Stabler asked, the exasperation evident in his voice.

"It's important," Shane responded and then quickly added, "Trust me, it's going to pay off."

He hesitated before he answered, but then Stabler said, "I'm sure I'm going to regret it but, okay, what do you need?"

"I just found out that my father died and I need a couple of days to make arrangements," Shane said. "Can you hold off talking to Andrews and Willard until I get back to Brantford? There are some things I want to check before Andrews knows he's in trouble and tries to use his money and influence on some of the other players in the case in order to either shut them up or cover for him."

"Sorry about your dad. I know that whole thing with him in prison has been tough for you," Stabler said sympathetically. "Sure, I can hold off. it's going to take time to review Mendez's statement anyway and I'll have to go over the situation with the Deputy Chief and likely the Crown Prosecutor."

Now, at the grave site, as had been the case since he found out his father was a murderer and was sent to prison, Shane's emotions ran the entire spectrum from love and respect for the man he thought he knew to resentment and hate for what his father had done.

He tried hard to concentrate on just the good times they had together, like watching westerns and debating who made the best hero, John Wayne or Clint Eastwood. There were those days after his father surprised him with the gift of the Charger that they would spend hours working on it together, and every afternoon when he walked into the shop after school, his father would be ready with a movie trivia question.

But keeping the good thoughts about his father front and center in his mind was very difficult because he would suddenly flash back to when he was seventeen years old and found Alina's body in that shallow grave in a woodlot and even worse, years later, finding his mother's body in the same area. No one should have to see those things.

"I have to say that I'm glad you changed your mind about burying your father by himself in another part of the cemetery," Emma said. "Even though you were so angry at him and could never forgive him, I think you would have regretted it."

"Yea, well, as far as he knew before he died, that's where he was going, and that fact was good enough for me," Shane said. "But after he died, I decided it wouldn't be fair to Grandpa and Grandma to not have their son buried beside them. And I recognized that I had blinkers on when it came to my mother and I had to accept the fact that what my father said about her wandering ways was probably true and that his anger and jealously over that drove him to do what he did. But, I will still never forgive him."

The trio stood looking at the coffin for a few more moments and then Shane said, "Let's get out of this heat."

Emma knelt beside the coffin and placed on top a single, stemmed red rose she had been holding.

They walked out of the cemetery and got into Emma's Jeep, which was parked on the gravel shoulder of the highway, and she started the vehicle and put the air conditioning on high so they could cool down.

"Fuck me," Ben said from the backseat. "When I was standing there, a lot of memories started flooding my head."

"Yea, me too," Shane said as he stared out the passenger window at the two cemetery workers as they began working around his father's grave.

"I was thinking back to everything that happened that summer when we were seventeen," Ben said. "I was thinking about when you got me to be the lookout while you broke into Max's house to look for clues about why his wife Alina disappeared. I nearly shit my fucking pants worrying that Max was going to come home and catch you. Fuck, you really took a chance that night."

It had been so many years since it happened, but hearing Ben talk about him breaking into that house brought it all back to Shane like it was yesterday. He remembered jimmying the lock on the glass sliding patio door at the back of the house to get in, a common method used by thieves to break in. Because of that, a lot of people put a metal rod or a wooden dowel in the inside track to stop the door from being slid open. The only way to get in from the outside would be to lift the door right out of the track, something that could be done if you knew what you were doing.

Why was remembering when he broke into Max's house have him thinking about patio doors? Shane then realized it was because it was a good way to get in without leaving any evidence of forced entry. There was no sign of forced entry into Farah Ahmed's house when she was murdered, a key point used by the prosecution in Barry Sterne's trial to show he had used his keys to get in.

Thinking about that while staring out the window of the Jeep had kept Shane quiet for some time, so Emma asked him, "Are you okay?"

"Yea, fuck, I'm starting to worry about you back here," Ben chimed in.

Shane turned to Emma and said, "Do you remember when we were talking about the Ahmed murder and you said maybe it was a case of Occam's Razor?"

"I do," Emma said. "I thought that when you looked at all of the players and their alibis, the evidence at the scene, and the circumstances around the murder, maybe the most obvious answer is the correct one, that Barry Sterne did, in fact, kill Farah."

"Well, when Ben mentioned my break-in at Max's house when I was seventeen, I started thinking about how I was able to do it without leaving a trace I was there," Shane said. "And that got me thinking about the one person who was around at the time of the Ahmed murder who, for some reason, nobody considered a suspect. I think the original investigators missed it because they were concentrating on Barry Sterne, Jackson Andrews, Rose Sterne, and even her daughter, Hanna. They all had alibis for the time Farah was killed eight years ago, and for when Sterne and Jason were shot."

"Sterne claimed he drove to Farah's house but didn't stay and then drove home where he was alone," Emma said. "He had no one to confirm his alibi, therefore making him the logical person responsible for the murder."

"But what if there's someone else who never had to supply an alibi?" Shane wondered. "I've been concentrating on breaking the alibis of the main players when I should have been applying Occam's Razor in a different way. If I believe Sterne didn't murder Farah and the other possible suspects all had alibis, then the obvious answer is the right one; the only other person with no alibi, a connection to the Sterne family, and knew how to get into Farah's house undetected."

Shane turned in his seat from facing Emma in the driver's seat to facing forward, put on his seat belt, and said, "I need to get back to Brantford right away. I know who murdered Farah and likely killed Sterne and wounded Jason, and I have to figure out a way to prove it."

Chapter Twenty One - 2016

Jason had to admit that the Crown Prosecutor, Shannon Renwick, did an outstanding job with her summation to the jury and it just added to his concern that he was unsuccessful in convincing some of the jurors there was reasonable doubt about Barry's guilt.

Renwick expertly made it sound like all of the evidence and testimony against Barry was indisputable and based on that, the jury's decision to find Barry guilty was straightforward. And guilty of second-degree murder, not the included lesser charge of manslaughter.

When Judge Paget called on him for his summation, Jason still hadn't made up his mind which one he was going to deliver; the long form he held as printed notes in his left hand, which would take at least half an hour to deliver, or the very brief one, a series of handwritten notes on a steno pad in his right hand.

In the end, he decided to go with what his gut told him, and when he stood up and walked to the lectern that had been set up facing the jury, he left all of the notes on his table.

"Ladies and Gentlemen," Jason began, "I realize that this trial has taken you away for over a week from your jobs and time spent with your families and you're anxious to begin your deliberations so you can go home."

"My colleague, the Crown Prosecutor, did a commendable job during her summation of trying to paint your decision as cut and dry, with no room for doubt about Barry Sterne's guilt in the murder of Farah Ahmed. Well, on my table over there, I have the notes for a rather lengthy summation where I would take you through the prosecutor's case step-by-step and point out its flaws and the multiple examples of where there's more than reasonable doubt about Barry's involvement in Ms. Ahmed's tragic death."

"But I have decided not to do that for the simple reason it's not necessary because you already know everything I was going to tell you and I would be belabouring the many points I have already made during the course of this trial."

"There's no murder weapon and the only evidence linking my client to the murder scene is his DNA in Ms. Ahmed's bedroom, where you would expect it to be since they were lovers. No forced entry? Well, we know there were members of Ms. Ahmed's family who had keys and we also found out during some of the testimony that Farah always left her key ring on her desk at work, so it would have been easy for someone to grab it during her lunch break and make a copy."

"Motive? Barry was prepared to come forward about his illegal accounting practices because he was deeply in love with Farah and that's what she wanted. He didn't feel threatened and as he testified, the only reason he was hesitating was because he was worried about the impact on his family."

"And then there's Eva Mendez who claims she and Farah were close friends and that Farah told her she was frightened for her life. But there's absolutely no corroboration that Farah felt that way and no proof that she and Ms. Mendez were even friends. The Judge ruled that what Farah allegedly told Ms. Mendez was allowed under the rules regarding hearsay, but I suggest you need to really consider Ms. Mendez's credibility."

"And you may also want to question the credibility of some of the other witnesses connected to my client and Ms. Ahmed. What if, unlike what they claimed on the stand, they did know about the affair and knew that Farah had damaging information about the firm's activities? That gives them the motive to silence Ms. Ahmed."

"So when it's all said and done, you and I both know this is far from the cut and dry decision the Prosecutor suggested. There's more than enough reasonable doubt for you to come back with a not-guilty verdict. Thank you."

Jason returned to the defence table and gave a reassuring nod to Barry. Judge Paget then gave his charge to the jury, outlining their responsibilities and some points in the law relevant to the trial. The jury was escorted from the courtroom just before noon to begin their deliberations.

Even with all of his experience in the courtroom, Jason wasn't sure how to answer when Barry asked him how long he thought the jury would take to make a decision. Instead of answering, he said, "If the jury comes back with a guilty verdict, I want you to know I believe there are grounds for an appeal and maybe I can get you released on bail until that happens."

"If I'm convicted, I don't want to appeal," Barry responded. "I don't want to go through this process again, it's too painful hearing about Farah over and over again. Jason, as far as I'm concerned you've done an excellent job for me in the face of everything that happened during the trial that, let's be honest, pointed to me as Farah's killer. Well, I didn't kill her, but I am responsible for putting her in the position that led to someone deciding she had to die."

"You can't think like that, Barry, you had no way of knowing that someone was prepared to murder Farah because of what she knew," Jason said.

"It's what I believe and I will never feel differently," Barry said. "When you combine that with all of the financial fraud I carried out, I deserve to go to prison. My mind is made up, Jason. If I'm found guilty, there will be no appeal."

The jury stayed out for two days, which both surprised and encouraged Jason because it meant they couldn't reach a unanimous decision on second-degree murder. Perhaps his efforts to establish doubt in the minds of some jurors about the veracity of Jackson Andrews, Bruce Willard, and Eva Mendez's testimony paid off, he thought.

On the third day, the jury returned with a verdict of not guilty of second-degree murder but guilty of manslaughter.

Jason was a bit confused by the verdict and thought perhaps it was a compromise the jurors made in order to get a unanimous verdict. Manslaughter in Canadian law is defined as the unlawful killing of another person without premeditation or intent. That means the jury believed that Barry did not intend to kill Farah when he drove to her house the day she was murdered.

After the jury delivered the verdict, Judge Paget thanked them for their service, ordered a pre-sentence report, and set a date for sentencing.

When the court was adjourned and before Barry was taken into custody, he and Jason shook hands and hugged briefly.

Jason said, "I'm sorry, Barry, I wish I had gotten you a better outcome. If you need anything, let me know."

Barry didn't respond and turned to watch his wife, Rose, and her father walking out of the courtroom without looking at him. His daughter, Hanna, who had been sitting in the gallery just behind them, stood up, tears running down her face, and stared at Barry.

"It's okay Hanna, I'll be okay, go and live your life," Barry said, his love for her obvious on his face.

"How am I supposed to do that when you've ruined it!" Hanna exclaimed then turned and walked away.

The Court Officer touched Barry gently on the arm to let him know it was time to leave. Barry watched as his daughter walked out of the courtroom.

"I'm so sorry," Jason heard him whisper.

Chapter Twenty Two - Present

As soon as he was back in Brantford from Port Elgin, Shane went directly to the office where Chioma Abiola was waiting to meet with him.

Shane had called Chioma from the Charger as he was driving out of Port Elgin and told her what he wanted her to do as soon as possible. They exchanged calls several times while he was on the road so Shane could get an update on her progress and Chioma could ask for any clarification on what she was looking for.

Emma had driven her Jeep Cherokee to Port Elgin and she said she would stay behind to check out of the motel and to complete any arrangements or payments at the funeral home in Paisley.

"I'm so sorry about your father," was the first thing Chioma said when Shane walked into his office and sat down. Chioma was sitting in a chair across the desk from him.

"Thanks, I appreciate that," Shane said.

"Are you sure you're okay to be doing this?" Chioma asked with concern in her voice. "You just lost your father."

"I lost my father a long time ago, Chioma," Shane responded flatly. "And now that he's dead, I can move on. So, what can you tell me about Corey Jones."

Chioma opened an I-pad she had on her lap and explained that Corey Jones was born and raised in Brantford to a middle-class family and attended Brantford Collegiate. He didn't do well in school and his records noted that he was diagnosed with learning disabilities. But he was quite smart when it came to hands-on work and tools, and his Guidance Councillor recommended he seek a career in the trades.

"I'm not going to ask you how you got access to his school records," Shane said.

"That's a good idea," Chioma said, smiling at him and then returning to the notes on her I-pad.

When Corey completed secondary school, he was unable to secure an apprenticeship but worked on several construction sites while he continued to submit applications.

"And in answer to one of the questions you asked on the phone while you were driving back to the city, yes, Corey at one point worked full-time with a window and door installation company," Chioma said.

"And that would include learning all about sliding glass patio doors," Shane said.

Chioma then explained that when work dried up in the local home building business, Corey took a job in the warehouse at Jackson Andrews' distribution company and that's where he met Hanna Sterne. He was twenty five years old and she was seventeen. They got married shortly after her father was charged with murdering Farah Ahmed and sent to jail to await trial.

"Why the interest in Corey Jones? Do you think he murdered Farah Ahmed?" Chioma asked.

"Not only that, but it's more than likely he shot Barry Sterne and wounded Jason," Shane replied.

"For some reason," Shane continued, "Corey fell between the cracks during the police investigation of Farah's murder and, I'm sorry to say, during Jason's defence of Barry Sterne. It's inexplicable that nowhere in the police notes that Jason got during trial discovery does it say that Corey was interviewed during the investigation. It's a huge miss by the police. Did they think Corey wasn't smart enough to commit murder? Did the investigators have blinkers on and only saw Barry as a suspect because there was no sign of forced entry into Farah's house? And, unfortunately, Jason missed it too."

"Well, he's not infallible," Chioma said flatly and in defence of Jason, which Shane expected and fully understood. She adored Jason because he took a chance and hired her, and was doing everything he could to help her fulfill her dream of becoming a lawyer.

"Why did you decide to focus on Hanna's husband?" Chioma asked

Shane said he'd been trying to figure out two things about Farah's murder. If Barry Sterne didn't do it, then how did the killer get into the house without leaving evidence of the forced entry and how did he, or she, manage to leave no trace evidence when they stabbed Farah multiple times?

"My friend, Ben, reminded me about a break-in I committed when I was seventeen years old and I was trying to solve a young woman's murder. I got into the house because I found a way to jimmy the lock on the patio door at the back of the house without leaving any marks," Shane said.

"Very clever," Chioma commented.

"Very lucky because there was no rod in the inside track to stop the door from sliding open," Shane said. "And that got me thinking about what I could have done if there was a track stopper and I wanted to get into that house without using forced entry. When I was at Hanna's house, I watched Corey re-install a patio door with no problem at all."

"But that was from the inside," Chioma commented.

"Yes, but there's a way to remove patio doors from the outside if you know what you're doing," Shane responded. "And thanks to everything being on the internet, I watched a YouTube video on how it's done. Have you ever seen those big, round suction cups with handles that glass installers use? You can buy them on Amazon."

"I can picture them," Chioma said.

"Okay, so here's what you do, if you know what you're doing," Shane said. "On the fixed panel, you remove the stationary brackets from the top and bottom and then use a screwdriver to loosen the tension bar on the inside of the bottom frame. You attach the suction cups, push up until the bottom of the door clears the track, then tilt the bottom out to clear the top track, and the door is out."

"You think that's how Corey got into Farah's house so there was no sign of a break-in?" Chioma asked.

"It's pure speculation, but makes sense given Corey's experience as an installer," Shane answered and then asked, "Did the forensics people take a lot of photographs or video while they were working in Farah's house, and were they included in the discovery material Jason received prior to the trial?"

"I didn't review them but there are photographs that were transferred to an electronic file," Chioma answered. "If I can use your computer, I can find them."

Shane got up and let Chioma sit at his desk and start working the keyboard on his desktop computer. While she was doing that, he got the chair that was facing the desk and put it right beside Chioma where he could sit and watch what she was doing. Within a minute, Chioma had found the file, opened it, and put the dozens of photos up on the monitor as tiles so they could quickly scroll through them and find the ones they wanted.

The forensics officers took a long series of photographs in the bedroom where Farah's body was found. But they also took photos to show the layout of the home, it only had one floor and a basement, and closeups of the front door and the rear patio door to show they hadn't been tampered with. Chioma found a shot of the patio door's floor track and it showed a metal rod in the gutter to the right of the inside sliding door.

"They took that picture to show that an intruder couldn't jimmy the lock and slide the door open," Shane said. "We need to see a photo of the entire patio door, if there is one."

Chioma used the wheel on the mouse pad to scroll through the photo tiles on the screen. She stopped, said, "I think this is one," and double-clicked on it to make it full screen.

"That's it," Shane said and then asked, "Is it possible to just isolate the glass in the stationary door?"

"I can try," Chioma said. She took a copy of the photo, put it into an image editing app, and highlighted just the stationary patio door.

"Shit, the photo would have been taken late morning or early afternoon, so there's a lot of glare," Shane said. "I need to see the surface of the glass."

"Hold on," Chioma said and started trying different light filters on the photo until Shane said, "Stop! That's it," and pointed at one area of the glass. "Do you see those?" he asked.

Chioma looked closely and saw two faint circle marks on the surface of the glass, spaced about a foot apart.

"Those were left by the suction pads on the glass handlers that Corey used to lift the door out of the tracks," Shane said.

"Wow! How did the forensics officers miss that?" Chioma asked.

"They didn't make a mistake because the rings are faint and it's something they would never think about looking for. They would be concentrating on dusting for fingerprints," Shane answered.

"I remember that on the list of fingerprints included in discovery, there were several lifted from the patio door handle and the glass around it that were marked 'unknown'. Any chance some belong to Corey and they're not on file anywhere?" Chioma wondered.

"Possible, but I doubt it," Shane responded. "He likely tried the sliding door in case it happened to be unlocked or if it was locked, considered whether it could be opened without leaving any marks. If he was being careful, he was likely wearing gloves and once he saw the security bar in the inside track, he would go ahead with his plan to remove the stationary door and the only thing he would be touching is the glass handlers."

"So, you've figured out how he got into the house undetected, what's next?" Chioma asked.

"The next question is how he managed to leave no forensic trace when he was in Farah's bedroom and stabbed her multiple times," Shane said. "I do have one rather out there idea and that's why I asked if you could access a list of companies that use Andrews' warehouse and distribution services on a regular basis."

"It's a long list, the company is very successful," Chioma said.

She pulled up another file on her I-pad and set it in front of Shane. "Is there something specific you're looking for?"

Shane started looking down the list and asked, "Does Andrews have any contracts with police, fire, hospitals, or emergency services?"

"Quite a few of them, actually," Chioma answered. "He handles importation, storage, and distribution to services across most of Southern Ontario."

Shane asked if it was possible to see a specific list of the equipment the company stored and distributed to emergency services and Chioma said that would take a few minutes.

While Chioma was busy on Shane's computer working her way back into Andrews' company's database, which he didn't want to know about, he went and got them coffee from the law firm's small kitchenette. He returned with two mugs and sat patiently drinking his coffee while Chioma did whatever she did to access the Andrews' files. Shane wondered, and not for the first time, how this wonderful woman sitting beside him had gone from a struggling law clerk who wanted to be a lawyer to an outstanding researcher and skilled hacker. He continued to be impressed by her talents.

"Okay, here you go," Chioma finally said as she reached out and turned the monitor slightly toward Shane so he could have a better look at the file. Shane went down the list and there it was! Another piece of the puzzle. He pointed to the company name Dupont and beside it, in brackets, Tyvek.

"There it is," Shane said. "How Corey avoided leaving any trace of himself when he killed Farah."

"What's Tyvek?" Chioma asked.

"That's the brand name of the special white coveralls that Dupont manufactures and are worn by emergency services personnel to protect them at sites where there are hazardous materials and by police at crime scenes so they don't contaminate any evidence."

"So you think that's what Corey wore when he was in Farah's house," Chioma said.

Shane replied that it would answer the question that if Sterne didn't kill Farah, then why were his hair and DNA the only forensic evidence found at the scene? Locard's Principle says there's always an exchange of material, sometimes only at the microscopic level, between a perpetrator and victim.

"Corey worked in the warehouse and could easily find a way to steal a Tyvek suit from the inventory to wear while he was inside Farah's house," Shane said. "The small backyard of the house was fenced in, six feet high, so Corey wouldn't have been seen as he put on the suit and worked to remove the patio door."

Chioma turned from the computer monitor, smiled at Shane, and said, "You're like Sherlock Holmes figuring this all out."

"Actually, Emma gets the credit for putting me on this path," Shane said. "She had said that sometimes the simplest answer is the right one. So, if Sterne didn't kill Farah and all of the other key suspects had alibis, who did that leave? Hanna's husband Corey Jones, the one person nobody thought about because he was always in the background, always quiet, never engaged."

"But what would have been his motive?" Chioma asked.

Shane then explained that the answer to that came during his visit with Hanna at her home when she told him she and Corey met when she was doing summer work at her grandfather's business. They were attracted to each other right away but Andrews was angry about the relationship because of the age difference.

"Probably the real reason was that Andrews didn't think Corey was good enough for his granddaughter," Shane said.

Hanna told him that her grandfather suddenly decided her relationship with Corey was okay and he went out of his way to take Corey under his wing, including paying for his training to be a tow motor driver, a substantially higher paying job in the warehouse.

"I believe the mentally bit slow Corey became a puppet and Andrews worked the strings," Shane said. "Andrews likely told Corey that if he wanted to be with his granddaughter then he would have to do some things for him."

Shane then told Chioma that Hanna's grandfather probably manipulated Corey into believing that he was looking out for him and that, no doubt, made Corey very loyal. Andrews then took advantage of that, telling Corey that Farah Ahmed was a serious threat to the family, including Hanna, and needed to be silenced. After he convinced Corey to kill Farah, Andrews would've told him they would set up Barry for the murder. Andrews likely even supplied Corey with the Tyvek suit.

"So does this mean that Corey also shot Barry and Jason?" Chioma asked.

"I'm assuming that, at this point," Shane answered. "I'm thinking that Andrews somehow found out that Barry wanted to appeal his conviction and Andrews convinced Corey it would be in his best interest if that didn't happen."

"So what now?" Chioma asked.

"I've got a couple of stops to make and then I'm going back to talk to Hanna and Corey Jones," Shane replied.

Chapter Twenty Three - Present

Jason pulled the Charger into the driveway of Jason Burke's north-end home, grabbed his cane, went to the front door, and pushed the doorbell.

Although he could easily afford a big house with lots of property and all of the amenities, Jason lived in a basic, two-storey, brick and siding house, on a small lot in an established neighbourhood.

Gillian answered the door, hugged Shane, and lead him into a family room off the kitchen at the back of the house where Jason was sitting in an easy chair with his legs up and a book in his hands. He was wearing lightweight track pants and a light blue polo shirt and Shane could see the deep purple bruise on the top of one hand where the IV had been inserted when he was in the hospital.

"I'll make some coffee," Gillian said and left the room.

"You look good," Shane said as he sat down in a matching chair beside Jason, separated by a small, narrow mahogany table.

"You're a terrible liar, Shane. I know that I look the way I feel. Shitty," Jason said with a thin smile on his face.

Shane told Jason about his trip to Port Elgin and his success in getting Eva Mendez to make a statement to police that she had been bribed to testify at Barry's trial.

Jason shook his head and said, "I knew she was lying right from the beginning, but I couldn't break her story and she was, unfortunately, very creditable on the stand. I should have tried harder. Thanks, Shane, good work."

Shane chose not to tell Jason about his confrontation with Mendez's boyfriend and son, but Jason did ask about Ben.

"I assume that if you were in Port Elgin you saw Ben Chen. How's he doing?" Jason asked.

"Same old Ben, still the center of his own universe," Shane replied and then added, "But below the foul-mouthed bluster and the front he puts on, I know that he's still deeply affected by what happened to him, particularly his time in jail."

"Completely understandable, it's going to take time for him to heal," Jason said and then, with a smile on his face, commented, "I sure hope you kept Ben away from Ms. Mendez when you were trying to persuade her to come forward."

Shane chuckled and said, "I made him wait in his truck."

Gillian came into the room carrying a tray holding two steaming mugs of coffee. Both men took it black, so she didn't have to bother carrying cream and sugar.

After Gillian left, Shane said, "I have a lot more to tell you, some of it you're not going to like, but I believe I know who really murdered Farah and possibly shot you and Barry."

Shane then outlined everything he and Chioma had found out since he returned from Port Elgin and after he had made sure that Eva Mendez's statement was in the hands of Brantford Police. Jason remained silent while Shane talked, didn't ask any questions, and the expression on his face didn't change until Shane was finished. That was followed by several moments of silence between the two men.

Then the look on Jason's face did change, to one that appeared to Shane to be a mix of both sadness and anger.

"Corey Jones. I can't believe I missed him," Jason said. "I was so focused on trying to discredit some of the main players, I never thought to check into him. A terrible mistake and it cost a man his freedom and then his life."

"Jason, you can't beat yourself up over this," Shane said firmly. "You're not the only one who never considered Corey a suspect. As far as the police were concerned they had the man responsible for Farah's murder. They had checked the alibis of other possible suspects but never looked at Corey because he was this quiet, kind of slow guy in the background, always working or at home with Hanna."

"It's still sloppy work on my part, no matter what others did," Jason said, almost in a whisper.

"Jason, I only got to Corey because I had nothing and no one else. It was a shot in the dark," Shane said.

"Don't try to make me feel better by trying to downplay what you've done," Jason said with some anger in his voice.

"So let's move on," he continued. "So you know how and why Corey killed Farah, but you have no proof to take to the police. Our only hope is that if the police arrest Jackson Andrews based on Eva Mendez's statement, he will implicate Corey."

"I don't think he will," Shane responded. "Andrews will likely accept his punishment for bribing Mendez but will claim he did it for the public good, to make sure that a guilty man was, in fact, found guilty. He's got too big an ego and a commitment to his own self-preservation to do anything else. He'll have some top-notch lawyers not named Jason Burke working to keep him out of jail."

"So do you have any thoughts on what can be done to get the right man arrested and clear Barry Sterne's name?" Jason asked.

"First, I want to talk to Bruce Willard, tell him what I've got on Andrews, try and shake him up a bit, maybe get his self-preservation to kick in," Shane said. "Then, I'm going to see Hanna and Corey Jones and take another shot in the dark, a hail Mary pass, and see if I can bluff Corey into believing I actually have evidence that will lead to his arrest."

"You're taking a big chance it'll work," Jason said.

"I have to try because at this point all I really have on Corey is pure speculation," Shane said and then got up from his chair and started to leave. When he got to the room's entrance, he heard Jason say, "Shane," so he turned and faced his employer and friend.

"Thank you," Jason said.

"You're welcome, but don't thank me yet because I haven't finished the case yet," Shane said with a smile.

After Shane left, Gillian came into the room to collect the tray and the coffee mugs. She saw that Jason's lips were pressed tightly together and he had a faraway look in his eyes. She sat down in the chair Shane had used and asked, "What's going on, Jason? What did Shane tell you that has you upset? Did it have to do with Barry's murder and what happened to you?"

"It's nothing for you to worry about, Jilly, really," Jason said to her with a rather weak attempt at a smile.

"Really? Nothing to worry about?" Gillian replied, exaggerating the words. "You're sitting there with a bullet wound likely connected to a seven year old murder trial and there's nothing for me to worry about? We've never kept secrets from each other and I don't want you starting now."

It was true. Jason and Gillian had shared everything during their marriage and when he was in the midst of a trial, Jason had come to rely on her unwavering support and insightful advice.

Jason then told Gillian everything that Shane had found out about the Farah Ahmed murder eight years ago, including Jackson Andrews bribing of Eva Mendez to have her testify at Barry Sterne's trial, which she was now recanting, the possibility the surveillance videos at Andrews' business had been altered, and the biggest news of all that Barry's son-in-law, Corey Jones, was likely hired by Andrews to kill Farah.

Gillian listened quietly as Jason spoke and saw how much it was hurting him to talk about a case she knew he considered his biggest failure.

"During the trial, I just knew that people were lying on the stand, but I couldn't prove it!" Jason exclaimed in frustration. "My gut told me that Jackson Andrews was behind everything; the accounting fraud to line his pockets, Farah's murder to stop her talking about what she knew, and framing Barry for her killing."

"You did the best you could with what you had," Gillian said.

"I didn't do enough to go beyond the police investigation and dig deeper into the various people connected to the case," Jason responded. "It was incompetent defence work, now even worse because Shane found out that no one, particularly me, didn't think to look at Corey Jones because everyone assumed he wasn't smart enough to be involved in the Andrews' family affairs."

Jason looked down at his hands for a moment and then said, "When Barry's trial ended, I just knew I didn't do enough for him. I let myself get distracted, I wasn't focused. I blame myself for the seven years Barry spent in jail and for his death."

Gillian leaned over, took Jason's hands in hers, and said, "Jason, listen to me, you're not to blame for what happened to Barry Sterne. I am because I made you continue with the case even though I knew you just wanted to be with me."

"No, Jilly, don't ever think that way!" Jason said, his voice cracking with emotion. "You were right back then. I needed to keep working or I would be spending my days making myself sick with worry. It was on me to put my personal situation aside and concentrate on saving a man's life. I realize now that I didn't do that."

Gillian could tell by the look on Jason's face that their discussion was over, for now. She leaned over, kissed him on the cheek, picked up the tray with the coffee mugs, and left the room, leaving Jason with his thoughts.

Chapter Twenty Four - 2016

Jason was pacing back and forth, something he didn't normally do when he was nervous, and then realized he was annoying the people who were sitting in the waiting room on the surgical floor of the Brantford General Hospital.

He stopped, looked at the faces of those who were staring at him, gave a thin smile and a shrug of his shoulders as an apology, and sat down in one of the uncomfortable chairs that seemed to be standard equipment in hospital waiting rooms.

The elderly woman sitting beside him, wearing a coat even though it was hot in the room and even hotter outside, patted Jason on the knee and said, "It's okay, dear, we're all worried. My husband, Jim, is having heart bypass surgery and he has a lot of other health complications that have me concerned he won't make it through. We've been married for fifty years."

The woman looked at Jason and he knew she expected him to reciprocate, which he didn't feel like doing to satisfy her curiosity, but he realized she was just trying to be friendly, so he said, "My wife has breast cancer, and is having a mastectomy."

"Don't you worry, dear, she's going to be just fine," the woman said patting Jason's knee again. "In this day and age, there's an incredible success rate in dealing with breast cancer. One of my cousins had both breasts removed ten years ago and she's doing just fine, so you don't need to pace."

Jason didn't respond, just crossed his arms and resisted the urge to get up and start doing what the woman said he didn't need to do. He was an emotional wreck and he knew it.

Jason met Gillian when they were both students in their senior year at North Park Collegiate. She was new at the secondary school after her family had moved to Brantford from Guelph and Jason had spotted her right away; a tall, slim, beautiful woman with short dark hair and green eyes.

He had asked around about her and found out her name was Gillian Saunders and then spent a week trying to get up the nerve to speak to her. Jason knew he wasn't an ugly guy, he wasn't worried about that, but he was shorter than Gillian and conscious of the fact he had a heavy build, and it wasn't from lifting weights.

By the end of the week, he decided he was ready and when he saw her standing by herself at her locker he walked up to her and said, "We're in the same Algebra class and I've been wanting to introduce myself. I'm Jason."

Gillian looked at Jason and said, "So formal. I've seen you in class. I'm Gillian."

"I know, like Gillian Anderson from the X-files," Jason said with a smile.

"Who?" Gillian responded with a questioning look on her face.

Jason's smile disappeared and he was sure he now had a look of panic on his face. Good move, Burke, you idiot! he thought.

"I'm just kidding!" Gillian said as she laughed. "I'm a big fan! Love the show! My bad, I didn't mean to make you tense."

"No problem," Jason said but believed it really was a problem if this girl thought he was a nervous goof.

"My friends call me Jilly and now you can too," Gillian said as she closed her locker and indicated they should walk together to their next class.

Jason and Gillian got married shortly after he passed the bar and now, all these years later, as he sat in the hospital waiting for news about her surgery, he couldn't fathom what he would do without her.

The lump in Gillian's left breast was found during her routine mammogram and a biopsy showed she had invasive ductal carcinoma, the most common type of breast cancer. It was advanced and while the surgeon thought it might be possible to save the breast with a combination of radiation, lumpectomy, and chemotherapy, his recommendation was to remove the entire breast and do the chemo.

The long wait for the surgery to be completed was excruciating and Jason was on his third cup of bad coffee when the surgeon, Dr. Malik, still in his scrubs, came to the door of the waiting room and got him. They went across the hall to a small, empty office and Malik said, "The surgery went well, with no complications, and your wife is now in recovery."

"That's great, thanks very much," Jason said, the relief evident in his voice.

"I do have to tell you, Mr. Burke, that there was a large area of cancerous cells in your wife's breast, but I'm confident I got it all with the mastectomy. Having said that, it's possible some pre-cancerous cells have spread to her lymph nodes. We will start her on chemotherapy in about four weeks to help ensure she is cancer free."

"Jilly's tough, she'll get past this no problem," Jason said, trying to sound confident.

"I have no doubt," Malik said and then added, "If you go back to the waiting room, a nurse will come and get you when you can see your wife."

Gillian's recovery from the surgery was painful and she realized there were going to be some bad days ahead once she started the chemo. Jason spent as much time with her as he could, constantly asking what he could do or get for her. Even though he was in the middle of preparation for Barry Sterne's upcoming murder trial, he was extremely reluctant to go to work.

Then one day, Jason came home, went into their bedroom where Gillian was resting on the bed, her head propped up with pillows, and told her that he was going to tell Barry, and inform the court, that he was withdrawing from the case.

"Why would you do that?" Gillian asked, the news taking her by surprise.

"I need to be here looking after you," Jason said. "You're going to need a lot of help once you start the chemo."

"No, Jason, I don't want you to do that," Gillian said. "I appreciate how much you care and I love you more than ever because of that, but you're a workaholic and will go stir crazy, and drive me crazy, if you hang around here all day."

Jason was sitting on the side of the bed and Gillian put her hand softly on the side of his face and said, "To be honest, I really need some time alone. I still haven't completely processed what has happened to my body. I have some things I need to work out and I can't do it if you're constantly hovering over me."

"I didn't know you were struggling, I just want to help," Jason said softly.

"I know, I understand that, but I have a nurse coming in and I have lots of people I can call if I need anything," Gillian said and then added, "Jason, you need to go to work because Barry Sterne needs you, you're an outstanding lawyer, and you're the best shot he's got. I will be fine and I will be here when you get home."

Chapter Twenty Five - Present

After leaving Jason's place, Shane drove downtown, parked, and walked to the section of Market Street where Barry Sterne's former accounting firm was located, now named Willard and Associates.

As he neared the entrance, he saw Bruce Willard approaching from the other direction, a briefcase in one hand and a takeout coffee in the other. Shane thought the man's tan was even darker than the last time he saw him.

When Willard saw Shane, he said, "I have nothing to say to you."

"Oh, but I've got a few things to say to you that you should hear," Shane said as he walked to meet Willard at the door.

"I can't imagine what those few things would be that I would care about," Willard said as he shifted his coffee to the same hand holding the briefcase and reached out to open the door. "I have a very busy day," he added.

"Well, we can stand here on the street while I tell you what I can now prove about your involvement in the conspiracy to frame Barry Sterne for murder, or we can do it in the privacy of your office. It's up to you," Shane said.

With his hand on the door, Willard stood and stared at Shane, who could tell that the accountant's mental wheels were turning as he tried to decide how to react to what he was just told.

"You better come in and explain why you're making such a wild accusation," Willard said and then held the door open for Shane.

Shane followed Willard as he walked through the reception area, ignoring the greeting from the receptionist, and into his office where he set his briefcase and coffee on his desk and sat down in his plush, expensive looking chair.

"Have a seat, Mr. Daniels, and explain yourself," Willard said in a tone that suggested to Shane that Willard was going to try and take control of the conversation.

"No, that's fine, I'll stand, this won't take long," Shane responded and then said, "I'm here actually to do you a favour. Eva Mendez has recanted her testimony at Sterne's murder trial and has given a statement to police that Jackson Andrews paid her to say that Farah Ahmed feared for her life because of what she knew about Sterne's illegal accounting practices."

"That's bullshit!" Willard exclaimed. "Mendez may have lied at the trial, but she did that of her own volition. Jackson had no reason to pay her, she likely did it just so she could get some attention."

Shane noted Willard's use of Andrews' first name, an indication the two had become more than just business acquaintances.

"Mr. Willard, it doesn't matter if you believe it or not," Shane said. "Andrews is going to be arrested and charged with criminal contempt of court for bribing a witness. It's now clear that Andrews was the instigator and knowing supporter of Sterne's manipulation of his business accounts and he had a lot to lose if that ever became public. He also knew all about Sterne and Ms. Ahmed's affair and that she was planning to notify the authorities about what she knew about what was going on with his accounts. Andrews felt threatened."

Shane paused to let what he said sink in with Willard, whose face had gone pale, even with his deep tan.

Shane continued by saying, "Andrews knew all of this because he had a great source at Sterne's firm. You. And please don't try and insult my intelligence by denying it. The police are going to come and question you, and probably arrest you for your role in what eventually led to Farah Ahmed's murder."

Willard stood up and said angrily, "Okay, I've heard enough of this bullshit! I don't know what your motive is for trying to drag me into something that happened eight years ago, but you can get the hell out of my office right now!"

Shane didn't make a move to leave and said, "My motive is to prove that Barry Sterne died an innocent man. I'm going to prove that Jackson Andrews hired someone to murder Farah Ahmed and let Sterne take the blame, and then had Sterne killed when he got out of prison and tried to kill his lawyer because he was worried Sterne was going to try to have his case re-opened."

Willard didn't say anything but did lean forward and put both hands on his desk to steady himself as the implications of what he was being told weakened his knees.

"What did Andrews give you to keep a close eye on Sterne? Money?" Shane continued. "What did he promise you after you told him about Sterne and Farah, and their plans to possibly expose him? What did he offer if you agreed to play dumb after Barry was arrested? This firm and his continued lucrative business?"

There was no immediate response from Willard as he continued to try and process what Shane was telling him.

Then he said to Shane, this time trying to keep his anger in check, "I need to speak to my lawyer and you need to leave like I told you."

"Listen, Bruce," Shane said. "I came here today to tell you all of this so that you have an opportunity to get ahead of it, to come forward and tell the police what you know before they show up here and arrest you. There's no statute of limitations on perjury in Canada and the maximum sentence is fourteen years. And if you get pulled into Andrews' conspiracy to commit murder, they throw away the key."

Shane turned and started to leave the office, but turned and looked at Willard who was still leaning over his desk, and said, "Think about it, but don't take too long."

When he got back inside the Charger, Shane looked at himself in the rear view mirror and was glad to see he wasn't sweating because he hadn't wanted Willard to see any signs he was nervous while he delivered his spiel to the accountant.

As he did with Mendez, Shane wanted Willard to believe that he had all of the proof he needed to show that Andrews was behind everything and to prove their complicity. The bluff worked with Mendez and he hoped it would do the same with Willard because, in reality, at this point, he had a theory but no evidence directly linking Andrews to Farah's and Barry's murders.

He hoped that if Willard came forward with what he knew, combined with Mendez's statement, it would be enough for the police to re-open the original case.

The next step was another visit with Hanna Jones, hoping he could bluff again and expose a killer.

Chapter Twenty Six - Present

When Shane called ahead to make sure Hanna was at home, she told him she would be on the patio at the back of the house when he arrived.

He didn't blame her for wanting to sit outside because it was a beautiful day with bright sunshine, clear skies, a temperature in the mid-twenties, and a light, cool breeze.

As usual, even with the windows open, it was hot in the Charger, and that always made Shane think of Emma with her 'no air, no way' policy when it came to going anywhere in the Dodge during the summer.

After he parked in front of her house, Shane walked along the side and into the backyard where he saw Hanna sitting in one of the cushioned chairs at the patio table, a tall clear plastic cup filled with ice and what looked like ice tea in front of her. They exchanged greetings and Shane sat on the opposite side of the table with the patio door to his left.

Hanna offered him a cold drink, which he declined, and they spent a few minutes talking about the weather, the always standard subject at the beginning of a conversation.

Hanna was wearing a long, patterned sun dress with her shoulders exposed. Shane noted her light complexion and thought about, compared to him, how cautious she must have to be when she's in the sun.

"So, what brings you by to see me again, more questions?" Hanna asked and then added, "It's a good time, my son's having his nap and Corey isn't home from work yet."

"I wanted to talk to both you and Corey, and I knew Corey wouldn't be home just yet, but I wanted to discuss some things with your first," Shane said.

"No problem, anything to help," Hanna replied.

"But Hanna, I want to tell you upfront that the things I want to ask and tell you, could be upsetting and you may not want to believe them," Shane said.

"This all sounds rather ominous," Hanna responded as she took off the sunglasses she was wearing and set them on the table. "Go ahead with whatever you have to say."

"You told me that your grandfather was very angry when he found out that you and Corey were spending time together," Shane said.

"He wasn't just angry, he was furious at me," Hanna said. "We had a big argument in his office, with him hinting, but not outright saying, that I shouldn't hang around with the hired help because they weren't good enough for me. I accused him of being a snob and discriminating against Corey because he was a bit slow."

"How did the argument end?" Shane asked.

"I think I already told you that I was a spoiled brat and normally got my way, but my grandfather was adamant and told me I'd have to find a summer job somewhere else if I didn't stop hanging with Corey," Hanna answered and then added, "He also suggested he would find a reason to fire Corey, which was the last thing I wanted."

"But then he suddenly changed his mind," Shane prompted.

"He did, and I was so happy," Hanna responded. "He said he was wrong to be angry and had misjudged Corey. He told me not to say anything to my parents about Corey and me, and that he would smooth things over with them when the time was right."

"Why do you think your grandfather changed his mind?" Shane asked.

"Look at me," Hanna said as she held her arms out at her sides. "Even my grandfather could see I was no prize. I was even bigger back then and there were most certainly no boys of my family's desired class and stature knocking on my door."

"On top of that," she continued, "I've always had trouble learning and understanding things, I got teased a lot in school because of that. It was one of the reasons that Corey and I felt a really strong connection to each other."

Shane leaned forward in his chair so that he was closer to Hanna across the table and said, "I have to tell you, Hanna, there was another reason why your grandfather suddenly decided it was okay for you to see

Corey and why he took Corey under his wing, training him for a better position and paying him a higher wage."

Shane then told Hanna that her grandfather had likely told Corey he could go ahead and date her, plus do better for himself, if he agreed to kill Farah Ahmed.

"What the hell are you talking about!? It was my father who betrayed me and murdered his whore girlfriend!" Hanna said loudly and angrily as she stood up, her hands clenched into fists.

Shane expected a reaction but this was the first time he had heard Hanna use such vitriol toward her father and Farah.

"No Hanna, your father didn't kill Farah," Shane then said firmly. "Your grandfather is about to be arrested for bribing a witness at your father's trial because he wanted to ensure your father was found guilty. And he did that to cover up the fact he manipulated Corey into breaking into Farah's house and stabbing her to death. And I believe I can prove that Corey did it."

This was Shane's bluff and he knew he was about to find out if it worked.

"I don't believe it! Corey is a kind, soft spoken guy who wouldn't hurt anyone! Hanna exclaimed, a look of anger, but also confusion on her face.

"What's going on?" Shane heard someone say and turned to see Corey looking at them through the screen on the patio door.

"Corey, thank God you're home!" Hanna exclaimed. "Mr. Daniels says he's got proof that you killed my father's girlfriend eight years ago. You have to come and talk to him and tell him he's wrong!"

"I'll be right there. I just want to make sure your loud voice didn't wake up Joshua," Corey said and disappeared from the screen door.

"You're wrong about Corey. He'll clear things up," Hanna said and while Shane anticipated an emotional denial from Hanna, he was curious why there was suddenly such a look of panic on her face. Did he miss something? Has she been lying and known right from the start what Corey did? Was she directly involved somehow?

Shane heard the screen door slide open and turned to see Hanna's husband walk out of the house and onto the patio.

It took a second for Shane to realize that Corey had a gun in his hand, which he raised and fired. Shane felt a rush of air as the bullet narrowly missed his forehead and he dived for cover under the table as Corey fired a second time. The bullet would have entered Shane's side as he turned to drop down, but instead it shattered the top of his cane, which had been leaning against the side of the chair, likely saving his life.

As Shane hit the surface of the patio, Hanna rushed up close to Corey, grabbed his wrist, and pushed the pistol aside before he could fire again.

"Corey! What are you doing!? Stop! How did you find my gun!? Hanna screamed.

Even in his shock as he lay under the patio table, Shane registered what Hanna just said. My gun? Hanna owned a gun?

Hanna was hugging Corey tightly and he lowered his arm and dropped the gun on the patio. Shane scrambled out from under the table, hooked the pointer finger on his right hand through the pistol's trigger guard, stood up, and backed away. He noted the gun was a .22 automatic.

Corey was sobbing, his head on Hanna's shoulder as she embraced him. "I was doing this for you! That guy was going to ruin everything!" He cried.

"Corey, you murdered that girl eight years ago?! You stabbed her so many times! Why? I don't understand!" Hanna said between her own sobs.

"I was in love with you and Mr. Andrews said I couldn't be with you unless I killed her and made it look like your father did it," Corey said. "He said nothing would happen to me, he would look after everything and we could be together."

After Corey said that, Hanna ended her embrace and used both hands to angrily push him away.

Then she screamed in his face, "I just killed my father for no reason because of you! I waited seven years to get my revenge for him wrecking our family and ruining my life, and he was innocent the whole time?! I shot his lawyer because he prevented my father from spending the rest of his life in jail where I thought he belonged!"

Hanna then began hammering her fists against Corey's chest. "Why didn't you tell me!" she screamed. "I shot my father for no reason!" she repeated.

Corey had retreated backward up against the side of the house as Hanna continued to pound his chest with her fists.

Shane was going to grab her in a bear hug from behind and pull her away, but first he called 911.

Prologue

As I was gathering up all of the paperwork and transferring various related files from my computer to a flash drive to go into a banker's box for storage, I was thinking that I should name the entire case 'The Big Bluff'.

I had to cross my fingers and bluff on several occasions because while I was confident I knew who did what and how they did it, I really didn't have any hard evidence.

I told Eva Mendez I had solid proof that she accepted a bribe from Jackson Andrews to lie at Barry Sterne's trial and because she believed me, she decided to come forward and make a statement to police about her duplicity. But, in reality, most of the proof would never make it to court because Chioma Abiola got it off the internet using some not very legal methods.

I told Bruce Willard that Andrews was going to be arrested for bribery and I was ready to prove the businessman hired someone to kill Farah Ahmed. I did have that theory, but that was about it.

As it turned out, Willard accepted what I told him and took my advice to get ahead of everything before the police came to interview him. I found out he was on his way, with his lawyer, to the Brantford Police while I was on my way to see Hanna and Corey Jones.

And then there was the biggest bluff of all, the one I used on Hanna.

I told her I believed I could prove that Corey murdered Farah which, at that point, was a bit of a stretch. With Chioma's help, I was able to discover some things that strengthened my suspicion, like the rings left on the patio door window by suction cups and the access Corey would have had to Tyvek coveralls, but none of that was proof.

If Corey had not tried to shoot me and had instead decided to walk onto the patio and deny murdering Farah, Hanna would have supported him and at that point, there was very little I could do about it.

Speaking about Corey trying to kill me, Hanna was surprised to see him with her gun, but probably not as surprised as me.

It was a Sig Saur, small and light-weight at seven inches long and seventeen ounces, and considered a great training weapon. Hanna said she bought it illegally from a friend seven years ago intending to kill her father and hid it, rather poorly, under some clothes in one of the drawers of her bedroom dresser.

I had assumed, which was a serious mistake on my part, that whoever shot Barry and Jason would have gotten rid of the weapon, but Hanna just returned it to the drawer and Corey came across it by mistake one day when he was putting away the laundry.

Corey wasn't sure at first what to make of Hanna owning a gun, but he didn't say anything to her about it and returned the weapon to where he found it. But then he read an online story, the information leaked from Brantford Police, that Barry Sterne was shot with a .22 calibre handgun.

Corey didn't know much about guns, so one day when Hanna was with their son at the daycare, he took the weapon out of the dresser draw and took a closer look at it. The gun was small and light with .22 etched on the side of the barrel and Corey realized what he was looking at. He put the gun back in the drawer and again didn't say anything to Hanna because he had his own terrible secret.

When he came home and saw me confronting Hanna, he decided he needed to kill me to protect her.

Jackson Andrews was originally charged with bribing Eva Mendez, but after Bruce Willard came forward with what he knew and Corey was arrested, a charge of conspiracy to commit murder was added.

Andrews, not unexpectedly, was defiant in his response to the charges, pleading not guilty. He immediately put together a team of high-priced, high-profile criminal defence lawyers and claimed he had no knowledge of Corey's involvement in Farah's murder and that Corey acted either at Hanna's urging or alone as a way of winning Hanna's affection.

Hanna's mother, Rose Sterne, hired a top defence lawyer out of Toronto to defend her daughter, who was charged with second-degree murder for killing her father and attempted murder for shooting Jason Burke.

Hanna's lawyer held a news conference and told reporters he plans to use the 'diminished responsibility' defence at her trial.

Under Canadian law, diminished responsibility or capacity reduces the charge from murder to manslaughter. The accused admits they broke the law but should not be held fully criminally liable because their mental functions were diminished or impaired.

I'm not sure how successful that will be in Hanna's case since she patiently waited seven years to take revenge on her father.

As for Corey Jones, Rose hired the lawyer just for Hanna, leaving Corey to apply for Legal Aide.

To complicate things even further, Jackson Andrews had previously paid a fine to settle any problems his company had with Canada Revenue, but now the CRA has decided to open a criminal investigation into tax evasion by Andrews' business and by him personally.

The RCMP is also now involved with questions about Andrews' banking practices and offshore dealings. I heard talk that many of Andrews' assets could be frozen, which begs the question of how he, and by extension Rose, were going to pay for the very expensive legal help.

There's no question the bottom line of all of this is that these cases are going to be tied up in the courts for a long time.

Andrews probably won't see a jail cell for the foreseeable future after being granted bail when one of his well-connected friends agreed to be his surety and he agreed to wear an ankle monitor.

I will have to testify at Andrews', Hanna's, and Corey's trials, but I'm pretty sure I'll need to update my suit before any of that happens.

Sgt. Mark Stabler of the Brantford Police Service was really put out with me for continuing to get involved in his investigation when I said I wouldn't and for putting my life in danger when I confronted Hanna and Corey at their home.

"For being such a smart guy, you sure don't think things through sometimes," Stabler said to me.

"How was I supposed to know that Hanna kept the gun she used to kill her father and that Corey would use it to try and kill me?" I said and then added, "When I went to their house, I was basically on a fishing expedition to see if I could get them to incriminate themselves."

"First of all," Stabler responded, "You said you went there knowing they were guilty but you were short on hard proof, so you should have known they might have reacted violently when confronted. As I said, dumb move for a smart guy. And secondly, you should have come to me first with what you had and I could have taken it from there, which is my job, not yours."

"That may be," I told Stabler, "However, look at what you've accomplished all at once. You've fixed a miscarriage of justice that occurred seven years ago and the real killer of Farah Ahmed is in custody, and you've solved the murder of Barry Sterne and the attempted murder of Jason Burke. Plus, you've taken down a corporate criminal by the name of Jackson Andrews"

"You did those things, not me," Stabler said.

"I don't need anyone knowing that," I told him and I meant it. Then I told him, with a big smile on my face, "Your name is on all the paperwork. You'll probably get another promotion."

Stabler didn't say anything, just shook his head at me, but I could tell from the expression on his face, including a hint of a smile, that he was also thinking promotion.

Emma was also not very pleased with me.

I had called her from the police station and given her a brief overview of what had happened on Hanna's patio and said I would likely be stuck at the station for several hours being interviewed and filling out witness forms.

Several hours turned out to be an understatement and it was deep into the evening by the time I got home. On the way there, I limped into a drug store and bought a cane to use temporarily until I could get another custom one made to replace the one damaged by the bullet from Corey's gun.

When I walked in the door of our house, Emma hugged me tightly and kissed me, and then said, "I could strangle you for, once again, putting your life in jeopardy. For Christ's sake, Shane, you've got to think about what you're doing before you put yourself in these situations!"

I chose not to tell her that Corey's first shot missed my head by inches because that would make matters worse. But I couldn't hide the fact that if weren't for my cane, I would have been shot in the side.

Emma calmed down, somewhat, and said, "I know you hate relying on a cane, but you have to admit that because you had it with you, it probably saved your life."

I smiled at her and said, "That may be, Emma, but I will always hate it."

The next day I drove to Jason's house and after the usual greeting and hug from Gillian at the door, I went and sat in the chair next to Jason and told him everything that happened.

"Your plan worked," Jason said after I finished. "Hanna reacted the way you hoped, but it was a miscalculation with Corey and it nearly cost you your life. I'm so sorry that happened."

"The thing is," I responded. "As I told the cops and emphasized to Emma, I was convinced that Corey not only killed Farah, but shot Barry and you because Hanna, or Jackson Andrews, told him that Barry planned to try and re-open his case. Corey wanted to prevent that from happening and being not a particularly bright person, he believed that killing Barry and his lawyer was the only way to do that."

"Perhaps you should have considered that if it was Corey, he wouldn't have been smart enough to get rid of his gun," Jason suggested.

"I agree, I should have thought of that," I conceded.

"You must have been surprised when it turned out it was Hanna, not Corey, who shot her father and me," Jason said.

"I really got that wrong," I admitted. "The clues were there if I had paid attention, but for the most part, Hanna never gave off the impression that she was harboring such deep hatred for what she believed her father had done. And her hatred never dissipated over the course of seven years."

I also explained to Jason that Hanna was supposedly volunteering at her son's daycare when Barry and he were shot, but the daycare operator has now admitted that she forgot Hanna had left for an hour saying she had an errand.

"Something like that, if I had known, would have definitely put Hanna at the top of my suspect's list," I said.

"I'm glad you weren't hurt," Jason said and then told me, "I can't tell you how much it means to me to clear Barry's name. As usual, you've done excellent work and I can assure you that you'll be compensated accordingly."

"That's absolutely not necessary," I responded. "I did it because I wanted to help you."

Jason never told me why he felt so strongly that he let Barry Sterne down at his trial. I had read the trial transcripts and I never saw any indication that Jason wasn't giving it his best effort in the face of evidence and testimony stacked against his client.

Jason did use the word 'distracted' a couple of times and I was never sure what he meant by that, although I wondered if there was something going on with him and Gillian at the time.

A week after what happened on Hanna's patio and I had completed several follow-up trips to the Brantford police station because they had more questions, Emma and I decided to get out of the city for a few days, mostly so I could decompress.

The weather was still hot so, as usual, Emma wanted to go to Port Elgin, sit on the beach, and enjoy the cool waters of Lake Huron.

We'll stop in at Ben's restaurant and, if he's there, listen to him rant in his colourful language about his latest pet peeve and his favourite subject of how no one should eat the food on his buffet, which is actually always very good.

On the way to Port Elgin, we stopped at Douglas Hill Cemetery, south of Paisley, to check on my parent's plot. We had ordered a headstone and wanted to make sure it was in place, which it was, a standard upright granite in a shade called Honey Rose.

Just my parent's names and dates of birth and death were carved on the front and as we stood there looking at it, the sun beating down on us just like the day we were there to bury my father, Emma asked, "Are you sure you didn't want some kind of inscription on the stone?"

"What would I put on there? 'Here lies my mother and father who I really did know'?" I replied.

"You knew the good things about them, Shane, maybe that's what you should concentrate on remembering," Emma said.

She was right with her advice, as always, but it will always be difficult to think about my mother's beautiful smile and loving hugs without flashing on her body, wrapped in a cheap blanket, in a shallow grave. Or remembering my father's easygoing manner and his love of cowboys and trivia, without seeing him as a convicted murderer, wasting away in a prison cell.

After we left the cemetery and got back on the highway, I started thinking again about the Barry Sterne case, specifically about his killer, his daughter Hanna.

After she was arrested, she told Sgt. Stabler that she wanted to kill her father before his trial started, but he was always either in jail or being escorted by a Corrections Officer. And she knew she would never be able to smuggle the gun through the security at the courthouse.

So she decided to wait until he finished his sentence and that's the thing I still have a hard time getting my head around.

 How does a young woman manage to hold on to her hate and her desire for revenge for seven years?

What mental flaw allows someone to go about their life juggling marriage, a home, and a baby, but still remain focused, year after year, on committing murder?

There's no question Hanna Jones was a perfect example of making revenge a dish best served cold.

Murder Sometimes Cold

Murray Moffatt